ALIEN HUNT

By the same author

Earth to Centauri series:
Book 1 The First Journey
Book 2 Alien Hunt
Book 3 Black Hole: Oblivion
Book 4 Civil War (Releasing in 2021)

Short story collections:
Deceptions of Tomorrow: Robots, Black Holes & Time Travel

'8 Down' from Saharanpur & Other Stories

धरती से सितारों तक:
भाग 1   प्रॉक्सिमा का रहस्य
भाग 2   एलियन हंट
भाग 3   ब्लैक होल विध्वंस
भाग 4   गृह युद्ध
'8 डाउन' सहारनपुर पैसेंजर: उपहास, रहस्य, रोमाँच और दहशत से भरी लघु कहानियाँ

Book 2

Earth to Centauri

ALIEN HUNT

By

Kumar L.

Earth to Centauri: Alien Hunt

First published in 2018.
This 3rd edition published in 2021 by Red Knight Books, an independent publishing firm.

Printed in India

Paperback ISBN 9789353822835

WWW.REDKNIGHTBOOKS.COM

Cover design by Aditi Shah (aditicshah01@gmail.com)

ABOUT THE AUTHOR

Whether you want to discuss faster-than-light travel, time travel, black holes or just the latest mobile phone, Kumar is your person.

He is a tech and social media enthusiast. He enjoys travelling and is fluent in several languages. A mechanical engineer who loves pulling apart gadgets and exploring their innards, he writes science fiction stories and tries to bring future technology alive in his books.

The First Journey is the first book of the Earth to Centauri series. It is easy to read and understand and is suitable for all age groups. The First Journey and Alien Hunt, the second book in the series, are both based on themes of adventure, thrill and drama, with a positive outlook at what the future may hold for humanity. Black Hole: Oblivion is the third book in the series with the latest adventure of Captain Anara and her crew.

His books have also been translated and published in Hindi.

You can reach him on
Twitter @Captain_Anara,
Instagram @KumarLAuthor,
www.facebook.com/kumarlauthor

Visit his website www.kumarlauthor.com to learn more.

GLOSSARY

Light years: The distance that light travels in one year. It takes eight minutes for light to travel from the Sun to the Earth, equal to about 9.46 trillion kilometers.

Faster than Light (FTL): Nothing can theoretically travel faster than light. However, all science fiction writers assume that this barrier will be broken someday and that humans will be able to reach the stars in FTL spaceships like *'Antariksh'*. Also known as relativistic speed.

Time Dilation: As an object travels at relativistic speeds, time slows down on the object when compared to a stationary observer. This is because time is relative and not absolute or fixed.

Alpha Centauri: This is the three-star solar system, which is closest to Earth at 4.2 light years. It will take us thousands of years to reach there with current rocket ships. Alpha Centauri A (Official name: Rigil Kentaurus) and Alpha Centauri B (Official name: Toliman) form a binary system, while Alpha Centauri C (Official name: Proxima Centauri) is around 0.2 light years away from AB.

Proxima B: A planet, supposed to exist in the Alpha Centauri star system circling the Proxima Centauri star. It may be suitable to support life.

Voyager 1: This was a space probe launched by the US's NASA on September 5, 1977. Part of the Voyager program to study the outermost reaches of our Solar System. Learn more here: https://voyager.jpl.nasa.gov

Golden Record: A 12-inch gold-plated copper disk engraved with sounds and images from Earth carried on board Voyager to share details of life on Earth with extra-terrestrials. https://voyager.jpl.nasa.gov/golden-record/

Radio Telescope: A special antenna that sends and receives radio signals from space.

Electromagnetic Waves (EM): Waves in electromagnetic fields like radio, microwaves, light, etc.

Goldilocks zone: A habitable zone near a star where the temperature and other conditions are suitable for life, like the Earth.

THE STORY SO FAR...

Book 1 - Earth to Centauri: The First Journey

In the year 2117, *Antariksh* became the first spacecraft from Earth to reach the planet HuZryss four light-years away, in the Alpha Centauri Tri-Star system. Its captain, Anara, discovers two worlds—HuZryss and KifrWyss. HuZryss is a desolate planet, except for one settlement of 'new humans'. These 'humans' were born from the embryos carried aboard the Voyager probe and raised by the reptilian civilisation of the planet KifrWyss.

Anara finds an enemy in the TrueKif, led by the enigmatic 'Chairman', who want to keep the KifrWyss reptilian bloodline pure. She and her team are held hostage on HuZryss, but they turn the tables on the Chairman with the help of nuclear weapons and a new ally, RyHiza, who is the leader of the ruling 'Discat' on planet KifrWyss. Anara and her crew return to Earth with three 'new humans'— who seek their help— Joe, Lucy, and her unborn child.

This is where 'Alien Hunt' begins....

AUTHOR'S NOTE:

The reptilian people from KifrWyss have been referred to by 'it' rather than 'he' or 'she' in this book, since they do not have gender differentiation.

CONTENTS

1

The planet KifrWyss (Alpha Centauri)

The TrueKif assault was as unexpected as it was ferocious. The defensive wall was easily scaled, the entrance breached in minutes. Flashes from explosions shredded the darkness, the screams of the dying breaking the silence. The shrieking of the prisoners, mixed with chaotic orders from the officers, shouted in panic, sent the sentries scrambling throughout the complex, unable to offer an organised defence.

The TrueKif slaughtered all the guards without remorse, using bullets, lasers, and finally knives. They moved on to the prisoners, killing them indiscriminately; warm blood flowed in rivulets. They spared none, save two. The complex was set on fire. Their first strike had been incredibly successful. The message to the Discat was clear. Do not underestimate the power of hate.

***

The Chairman seldom had reason to smile, but it had to

admit that the campaign was close to giving it one. Very soon the Discat would be overthrown. War was inevitable. Very soon it would rule the land from the West Ocean to the Edge of the East. It had taken years of preparations, but the time had finally come to deliver the people of KifrWyss.

And yet it was not happiness, satisfaction, or anticipation that filled its heart. No; the burning, acrid desire for revenge saw to that. The Chairman could not abide humiliation, and so the people of Earth would not endure what was about to be unleashed on them. Not vengeance; but justice. Justice for what they had done to HuZryss. Never had the prospect of justice tasted so very delicious.

The mercenaries were free. The moment was close.

Perhaps, the Chairman supposed, it had enough reason to smile after all.

***

The Chairman prided itself on its hideout. Set within the mountains of the continent, buried in the depths of a vast jungle, only a handful of trusted TrueKifs knew of its existence and fewer still knew where its exact location. From the outside, and especially from the air, it was undetectable. Inside it was a veritable palace, full of everything the Chairman could desire to be comfortable.

Surrounded by opulence, standing on a raised platform looking down at the two people so crucial to its plan, the Chairman had scarcely felt so powerful or at ease. Those things came with knowing that it was in control. It had detailed out every contingency and provided for every eventuality. The plan was infallible, and the only thing left was to convince the two individuals of the fact. Everything depended on their complete and total devotion to the cause of the TrueKif. The Chairman had chosen them carefully; a burning desire for revenge, reinforced by an utter lack of fear or compunction in taking a life.

The disgrace of having lost out to the Earth people, the outlanders, on HuZryss blazed deep in its heart. The capture of its team and their short, public trial had added insult to injury. But it had freed them. The war had just started, and it was pleased with the initial success. The battles would be bloody and great sacrifices would be required and the Discat would have to pay. The time had come for the TrueKif to come out of the shadows and seize power. It may be many months before it could seize the capital. Meanwhile, there was one more vital task to be accomplished.

The Chairman's voice filled the room, echoing from the gilded walls as it addressed the two. "I have raised you. I have rewarded you. I have bestowed much on you since birth. Now, the payment has come due." The Chairman paused, watching them. There was no visible reaction from either of them. "However, not every payment is painful," the Chairman continued. "Yours will be that of a monumental task, one replete with honour and privileges should you succeed. I will not lie; it is a dangerous task. It requires the utmost cunning and bravery. If you succeed, your name will be legendary on KifrWyss and there is nothing worth more than receiving honour from the loyal citizens of KifrWyss." It paused again, letting the message sink in. Still no reaction. It was time to roll the dice.

The two kept their heads bowed; faces obscured as they listened in silence. The Chairman walked, moving down from its platform to circle the two figures. It could smell their fear now; fear of the raw power emanating from the Chairman.

That was good. The Chairman could use fear, especially when that fear was bolstered by the awe they must be feeling. It was virtually unheard for people to be brought into this room to meet the Chairman face to face. For them, the mission itself would guarantee immortality.

"The outlanders," the Chairman infused that word with all the spite it could muster, "from Earth defiled our home when the probe we retrieved brought their foul seed to HuZryss. Now they have sullied it with rank humiliation, bringing a ship, lording over us and holding our people hostage. And what does the Discat do? Punish them? Execute them? NO!" It stopped right in front of the two, trembling with rage. "NO! The Discat gave them fame in the very same hall where our noble ancestors have met for generations. The Discat is full of foolish and old creatures; easily seduced by the offer of friendship from a planet they deem exotic. And RyHiza - the biggest fool of them all. It believes that these outlanders will make it stronger! It is imperative that I make everyone understand the TrueKif will NEVER accept this; that we will fight to the last person to keep our lines pure!"

Still, the two did not raise their heads or say a word. They understood. It was more than their life's worth to express anything except complete obedience in the Chairman's presence.

It spoke quietly now, each word barely more than a hiss. "I will send a message to Earth so deadly that the mere mention of the word 'TrueKif' will turn them into mewling children. I will show them my power; strike them deep in their homes until they feel my wrath for having contaminated my planet." It smiled, baring rows of sharp teeth. "And today I have the means to fulfil this. You two, my brave emissaries, will go to

Earth. Carry out my orders, and upon your return, you will be heroes. You will have the wealth and power few to even dream of."

The Chairman could now see the smiles on their faces, and its satisfaction grew.

"In secret, we have built a ship - a ship with capabilities unknown to most. More powerful and more advanced than anything that's ever been built. This ship will have only one purpose, and that is to see you to your destination. You will have a small crew to assist you. Once on board, you will get detailed plans. From there, I demand of you only one thing. For your sakes as much as for anyone else's." It came to a halt directly in front of them. "DO NOT FAIL ME!"

Then, all that was needed was a wave of the hand, and the two were gone, bowing themselves out of its presence.

***

PiYena, the Chairman's assistant, waited for them outside the door. Swiftly it ushered them down a hall and into a room. It was only as the door closed that the two allowed themselves to raise their heads and look at PiYena.

"I will come straight to the point," said PiYena. "You will launch in two days, with six crew members to pilot the ship. Your weapons will be on board; you will learn to use them on the way. Make no mistake, this mission is deadly, and you need to be thoroughly prepared if you are to have even the smallest chance of success. You will devote your time on the ship to this purpose alone. From now on you will only be referred by your designations; Jur and Biw. One and Two. The secrecy of this mission is paramount."

Jur glanced at its companion. "But PiYena... we know nothing about Earth. And even less of what we are supposed to do there. How-"

"Shall I report your doubts to the Chairman, Jur?" PiYena asked. "Or the implicit disrespect of your questioning? You will have help as soon as you land. Someone will wait for you there. He will take you to your destination. And as to your task - it's elegant in its simplicity. You will deploy a device so formidable it will annihilate entire cities and teach humans something their arrogance has blinded them to," PiYena grinned. "And that is to never approach us again."

2

Antariksh

The ship flew onwards to Earth: sleek, dark, silent and invisible. It had left HuZryss far behind, but there were still a few light years to go before it reached home. Inside *Antariksh* and on the planets it had left behind, the turmoil of human and alien emotions threatened to break through the thin veneer of civilized actions.

***

Lucy screamed.

She had another nightmare. The same nightmare. She was still in the middle of this nightmare, if only for a few seconds. It took her a moment to stop thrashing, catch her breath, and remind herself that the darkness surrounding her meant she was no longer in the place she used to call home. She would soon be on Earth, away from the TrueKif, away from their ubiquitous menace, even if it did little to make her feel better.

'Lights', she reminded herself. She was supposed to say 'lights'. She whispered it, then a little louder when she realised the AI had not heard her. The room brightened, and she slowly exhaled. The lights didn't eradicate the nightmare, but they made her feel better, if only for a short while. She didn't feel quite so afraid.

She placed her hand on the gentle swell of her stomach, reminding herself that she wasn't alone. Not anymore. Not with the reason she was going to Earth. Anara was also at her side, as was Joe and the doctor. *I am not alone. My heart may be broken, but my daughter will be my anchor. She will receive the love of her people, not the hatred of the TrueKif.*

She lay back on the pillow, trying to get comfortable, needing the sleep to keep up her strength - Dr. Khan had insisted on that. Never having experienced or witnessed childbirth or having had a parent of her own, Lucy had learned to listen and follow carefully whatever the doctor told her to do. In the end, her daughter needed to be born healthy and tough. Anything less would not do for the firstborn of the HuZryss.

***

In another part of the ship, muffled sounds floated out of a room. His wounds had opened again. Major Rawat could feel the fresh blood inside his boxing gloves, its horrible wet warmth coating his fists. But he didn't stop. The pain was fuel, fuel for his anger, fuel for each strike against the bag. Maybe, if the pain was terrible enough, it would drive the mission from his thoughts and nightmares. Perhaps he didn't deserve the pain. But it was a part of him now.

He kept punching.

It was so easy for Captain Anara to make noises about diplomatic victories. As if those hollow words meant a damn thing to those who had spent three days in captivity. As if those words could make up for the sleepless nights and the dreams that came when he did eventually fall asleep. His team had been called elite soldiers. It was a cruel joke. Nothing about their conduct had been elite. Calling them herded, helpless cattle would have been too kind. The TrueKif on HuZryss had dominated them, held them hostage, and he had been impotent to protect his people.

Never again, Rawat promised himself. With every punch, he said the words to himself. Never again. One more chance to even the score with the TrueKif was all he needed. For that, Rawat would have sold his soul to the devil.

***

The crew was still coming to terms with the events of the past year. The attacks on their ship, *Antariksh*, by the alien ship of the TrueKif, the subterfuge with the nuclear weapons. Finding humans 4 light years from Earth. The secret carried aboard Voyager. The attack on their ship by TrueKif. Their retreat having to leave hostages behind. And finally, the friendship of the people of the planet KifrWyss and their charismatic leader RyHiza. It was all behind them. They were on their way back home. The terror of having been ambushed in space was giving way to the acceptance that life on Earth had changed.

After decades of searching, humankind had contacted an alien civilization. They had found life on not one but two planets besides Earth. The crew on-board *Antariksh* were heroes.

***

The ship was now within the Oort cloud on the outer fringes of Earth's solar system. The journey back from Alpha Centauri had been uneventful. *Antariksh* had continued to make excellent progress, eating away the light-years of distance, interlacing Jumps at the speed of light with the more sedate cruising velocity.

The Captain had taken her deputy, Commander Ryan's advice to heart and was seen more often roaming around the ship than she was seen in Ops. Her interaction with the crew had significantly increased. The excitement of the contact with the KifrWyss and finding human beings on another planet was still alive. She had encouraged the crew to chronicle every aspect of the trip from their viewpoint. Indeed, now that most of the team was involved in cataloguing the information and connecting the dots, fresh revelations were cropping up.

For instance, the similarity in DNA patterns of species on two different planets separated by many light years, Earth and KifrWyss, was uncanny. Scientists on both planets would spend years trying to unravel this mystery. To Anara, a scientist at heart, this proved that evolution worked in similar ways. Any planet that has the ingredients necessary for life - water, oxygen and a suitable temperature - would eventually give rise to living organisms. The only variables would be time, measured in eons, and possibly external factors that resulted in a species becoming dominant. Bipedal mammalian humans rose on Earth, and reptilian life achieved sentience on KifrWyss.

However, a thought kept nagging her at the back of her mind - isn't it still possible that this DNA had been planted on the two planets by some other beings? Life on two planetary systems so close to each other in this vast galaxy was just a tad bit mysterious. Just like Voyager 1 had carried human DNA to a distant planet, wasn't it probable that other alien probes had carried DNA to both Earth and KifrWyss and then evolution had taken over? This was a question theologians of various religions had debated on Earth for hundreds of years. Maybe this was best left to them to resolve.

She was happy to have played a minor role in finding and making friends with a new species. And even better - they were bringing back two of the 'new' humans to Earth, and one of them was pregnant. This will blow her boss, Director Srinivas's mind for sure, she thought.

She and her crew had been wholly devoted to the care and coaching of Joe, Lucy, and the unborn child. Dr. Khan, the head of medical, was like a lioness protecting her cubs, when it came to the welfare of the two people. In the beginning, he had allowed them minimal contact with the crew, confining them to the medical bay in protective areas while he checked out their immune systems. After all, they couldn't wear sterile suits forever. Their bodies had never been exposed to any diseases from Earth. The last thing he wanted was that the first family coming back to Earth, from HuZryss, caught a virus and perished.

He had built up their resistance through a careful regime of inoculations and controlled exposure to the ship's environment. Everyone meeting them went through strict decontamination protocols. Every bit of air was cleaned through high-efficiency filters, and the food and water were synthetically prepared. His efforts had born fruit, and he was confident that Joe and Lucy would be sufficiently prepared for life on Earth by the time *Antariksh* landed. Though, to be on the safe side, he would have still preferred another period of quarantine.

Anara had set up a roster, enabling every person of her crew to interact remotely with the couple. This would help Joe and Lucy to polish their language skills and prepare them to be better assimilated. They were also being given lessons in history and culture to help them get a better understanding of life back on Earth. Anara was sometimes afraid that bombarding them with vast amounts of information may be too much for the couple to handle. But they had surprised her with their voracious appetite for knowledge.

In the meantime, Commander Ryan had been working on preparing detailed reports on every aspect of KifrWyss technology and society. Dr. Lian, head scientist, was preparing dossiers on the planetary systems they had visited and supplementing them with copious amounts of images and samples. It would take years for the best researchers on Earth to run through all the data being brought back and form a comprehensive understanding of the Alpha Centauri star system.

The head of engineering, Madhavan and security in charge, Major Rawat, were devoting their time analysing records of their military engagements against the KifrWyss building up a database of their ships and weapons systems. The KifrWyss technology differed from that of the Earth ship. Their propulsion system had enabled them to achieve similar FTL (Faster Than Light) speeds. But instead of longer Jumps, the KifrWyss relied on 'skips', as Madhavan had taken to call them - interspersed FTL and cruise speeds of durations shorter than that of *Antariksh*. Madhavan was hoping to combine the two technologies to increase the sustained Jump time for Earth ships.

However, the KifrWyss were using nuclear reactions with an unknown element that provided adequate energy along with matter-antimatter reactions. But they had not explored making weapons of mass destruction using fusion or fission reactions. Additionally, their method of producing energy left behind deadly radiation. Their reptilian physiology made them somewhat immune to it. But for humans, even short-term exposure to this radiation would be fatal.

There was one common theme running throughout the ship–the crew's desire to get back home and hear the voices of their loved ones. They were eagerly looking forward to being able to access messages stored in the communication buoys as they neared Earth.

3

2118, The Present Day

Manisha straightened her back, trying to work her tired spine, which troubled her despite the comfort of the adaptable seating. She knew she would have to call the captain eventually, but she needed to have something concrete to report. Three hours had passed since she had started trying to lock onto the weak signal detected by the ship's sensors.

Her hours of work bore fruit as there was a muted chirp from her console, and the lines on her display firmed up. *Finally,* she thought, *time to call in the cavalry.*

"Ops to the captain. Ma'am, we're receiving a message," Manisha said over the intercom, interrupting Anara's planned morning routine of yoga and calisthenics.

"Anara here, Manisha," the Captain acknowledged, somewhat surprised. "Are we in range of the signal buoys already? I thought we were still a couple of weeks away."

"No Captain, we're still not in range of the signal buoys. I… I think you'd better come up to Ops. I can't explain it over the intercom."

Why was Manisha being mysterious about a message transmission? This was good news, right?

"Okay," replied Anara. "I'll be there in a minute. Better call Ryan and Rawat too."

Anara rapidly packed away her kit. As she exited the exercise room, she ran straight into Ryan.

"What's this message Manisha was referring to? Something from Earth?" he asked.

"I don't know, Ryan. Do you think ISC has found a way to reach radio signals this far out in space?"

Ryan shrugged. "They've been working on it for a long time. They might've cracked it by now."

The door to Ops opened, and they entered together. Manisha looked up from her station.

"Captain, I'm sorry about disturbing you. But I can't make sense of it."

"It's alright, Manisha, let's look at what you've got," said Anara as she walked over to the station. "Walk us through."

"Yes, ma'am," she said, pulling up a display. "A few hours ago, our system detected electromagnetic signals directed towards our general position. But it was not something we used to communicate in space. The wavelength is too long, and the input time is prolonged. I'm only able to get one letter every minute or so."

Anara and Ryan examined the display closely.

"Okay, go on. What's the source of the signal? Earth?"

"No, Captain. It's from the opposite direction—from Proxima."

Anara raised an eyebrow in surprise. "Let's see what you've retrieved so far."

The central main display screen came alive and as each

letter came in it was displayed in a sequence.

"Narada, resolve the message please," Anara instructed the ship's artificial intelligence.

"Working. Now displaying on screen 2."

The letters formed words - *This message is for Captain Anara on Antariksh from…*

"That's all we've received so far." The anticipation in Ops increased exponentially as the next word was revealed.

This message is for Captain Anara on 'Antariksh' from… *RyHiza.*

"Wha…!" exclaimed Anara, completely caught by surprise. The last thing she'd been expecting was to hear from the leader of KifrWyss. "What the hell is this all about?"

"There are more letters coming in, Captain," Manisha called out.

The screen continued to present the message letter by letter, arranging them into meaningful words. It took several minutes before the entire message was downloaded and then the signal started repeating all over again.

This message is for Captain Anara on 'Antariksh' from RyHiza. Very important. War on KifrWyss. The TrueKif have attacked the capital. We are defending, but the situation is not good. One ship with the enemy is on its way to Earth to destroy. I cannot help you. I ask you to save our friendship. Save me. Save KifrWyss.

The silence in Ops could have been cut with a knife.

"What has happened on that damn planet since we left? It hasn't even been six months," said Anara angrily. *This was a direct appeal for help from KifrWyss. What did RyHiza mean about the ship destroying Earth? Was that even possible? Why? This was madness. What am I going to do about the enemy ship? Chase it across the solar system and blast it into space? Yeah, right!* She remembered how the last two encounters had ended. *Antariksh* had turned tail and ran away at full speed.

"The situation has transformed since we left, Captain. The message must be a few weeks old at least. I wonder what the state of the planet is now." Ryan wondered.

"Ryan, this is a complete disaster! Even before we have cemented our contacts, our friendship seems under threat. And you know what? I'm pretty sure that somehow we caused this mayhem."

"Do the KifrWyss have ships powerful enough to get to Earth? I thought they had only three ships and the space exploration program had been deliberately slowed down over the last many years," Ryan looked at the team for confirmation.

"I thought so too, but it looks like we were wrong. On KifrWyss, RyHiza clearly stated that they had only three ships, one of which it was using. The TrueKifs had stolen one, and we had recovered the last. Where did this fourth one come from?"

"I guess we will find out when we find the ship. What are the chances that this signal is a fraud?" asked Anara.

"We've no way of knowing that, Captain. Except for the fact that it's addressed to you and RyHiza's name is attached, there are no other identifiers. Someone could have taken over the radio telescope on HuZryss and may well be sending us a false signal," replied Ryan.

"We must proceed on the assumption that the signal is genuine, ma'am," said Rawat. *I've had enough of these games. If the TrueKif want a fight, we should give them one.* "They must have some powerful people behind them to be bold enough to attack the capital. I wouldn't put it past them to have built another vessel. One that can reach Earth."

"Humph. Too many ifs and buts. There'll be more than enough time for speculation later, people. Let's focus. We need to decide now. Do we go back to Centauri to help RyHiza, or do we continue back to Earth; to safety - ignoring RyHiza's plea for help? Or do we search for this ship?" asked Anara.

"It's pretty clear to me - we must get to Earth. We've got to warn people and prepare to protect the planet. Our signals will not reach Earth of time, but maybe we can," said Ryan.

"No. We must search for the ship and destroy it before it even reaches anywhere near our home. Once it enters the solar system, no one can predict what they'll do," said Rawat. *And after that, we will go to Alpha Centauri and seek the cowardly TrueKif.*

"No way, Major. We must get to Earth as fast as we can," repeated Ryan. "However much we try to pretend, we're not a warship, dammit. We can't go gallivanting across space to search for one ship. Where would we even start?"

"We cannot go back to Earth, Ryan! Don't you see what is at stake here? Two planets will be at war if we don't act now and do something about it!" Rawat was livid. *How could they run away from a fight?* "We've got to find that ship and then maybe we can go back and help RyHiza." Rawat's position was apparent, and he was itching to pay back the TrueKifs for having kept them captive for so many days on HuZryss.

"I know you're gunning for a fight with the TrueKif, Major, but this is not the time. You may be a soldier, but most of the crew of this ship isn't. And tell me, what is the guarantee that there will be anything left to save by the time we reach Centauri? Huh, Rawat? What's the guarantee? It'll take us months to get there, and we are only one ship. We are one ship against God knows what the TrueKif would have brought to the fight. Going back would surely be suicide for *Antariksh* and the crew. And for what? Your pride or your bruised ego?" pushed back Ryan.

The major glared at him, his hands balling into fists. Then he took a deep breath and allowed his hands to relax. Ryan's logic was sound.

Anara was torn between her desire to help RyHiza and trying to prevent a mercenary attack on Earth and the consequence of a full-blown interstellar war. The situation has unravelled so suddenly. Earth would be caught off guard; unprepared. Billions of lives could well depend on her decision as commander of the mission.

She shook her head and raised her hand, closing out the exchange of words between her senior staff - ending the argument before it could go any further. Her two deputies were poles apart, though both were making valid points.

"All right!" she said, raising her voice. "I hear both of you, but do we really have a choice? We can't be playing superheroes, can we?"

Anara reached her decision. Her path was clear. "The crew is tired; *Antariksh* is not designed for this mission. We'll only get ourselves killed if we go back now. We must get to Earth and warn them about the danger. Then we'll leave it to the professionals to handle the situation. We are astronauts, not soldiers. So, let's behave like it."

She looked around Ops and ran through a mental checklist. "What we need right now is to reach Earth as fast as we can to deliver the warning. Let's concentrate on that."

***

"What did RyHiza mean when he said, 'destroy Earth'?" wondered Ryan as *Antariksh* prepared for the next Jump. Over the last week, we have pushed the ship to its limits. The Jump cycles were getting longer, and they had stretched the crew; both the team and the ship's systems were rapidly reaching their breaking points. Half the status boards across Ops were in the red or amber zone.

"I'm not sure, Ryan. A super-weapon or mercenaries would be my guess. This is out of my league. I've started realising that there's much more to being a star ship captain than simply flying this bucket of bolts," replied Anara, ruefully. "Just look at what we've been through in the last year: we've contacted an alien civilisation, been shot at, held hostage and escaped by the skin of our teeth. None of the training scenarios prepared us for this, right? And now we have an additional threat - a ship aiming to destroy Earth. At the very least, this will create an atmosphere of mistrust and fear. That would play right into the xenophobic hands of the TrueKif. What troubles me even more is - how would TrueKif even expect to carry this out? I mean, besides whatever they would've learned from us and the Voyager probe, Earth is unknown to them. How do they even expect to survive there even for a few days? It's just not the air, but food, water, even navigating a strange planet."

"I agree it seems impossible. Even the mere thought is farfetched. We ourselves took two decades to advance this far," said Ryan. He suddenly seemed to realize something and turned towards Rawat. "Major, did we detect any attempts to access the ship's records while we were on HuZryss?"

"You mean unauthorised access? I don't think so. We have multi-layered protection across all systems. There've not been any alarms. I'd assume that it would be beyond their capabilities."

"Have you already forgotten Major," said Ryan drily, "that we broke the codes on the telescope and turned it against the KifrWyss?"

"I've not forgotten anything, Commander," said Rawat acidly, "and thanks for reminding me again." He, however, recognised the truth behind the question and nodded grimly. "I'll ask Narada to examine the records again. Maybe we should also check with the crew if they left any data behind."

"Won't hurt to ask," agreed Ryan.

Anara observed the exchange between the two men. She understood that their mutual respect was still in place - notwithstanding the heated exchanges and sarcastic remarks. The ship was in expert hands. Now if only she could get her message across to Earth to prevent a catastrophe.

The Prime Minister's Office, New Delhi

The call from Minister Balraj had been short. The minister did not expect *Antariksh* to return. The PMO itself had been expressing increasing anxiety at the lack of communications from *Antariksh*, and Srinivas had been summoned to the PMO for the second time in two weeks. This was unexpected and had not happened for many months, ever since *Antariksh* had left on its journey. He had been providing regular, monthly updates to the PMO, but with nothing new to report, this had become routine if not downright mundane. But not this time. He wasn't sure what was to be discussed this time even though this was, undoubtedly, his mission. As the head of the ISC or Indian Space Command, he was the person who had worked on sending India's first interstellar mission to Alpha Centauri on the ship called *Antariksh*. Now, as he waited outside the cabinet room, he felt like a disobedient child being called to the principal's office again and again.

There was still no news from *Antariksh*. While this was understandable, given the light-years of distances involved, he was getting worried. He had expected to receive some more alien signals from the planet Proxima in the intervening time but the GMRT telescope had reported no new incoming transmissions. The cosmos was quiet.

He berated himself for not having pushed harder to get the faster-than-light radio-transmission project team delivering on its promise. Without FTL signalling, he had no means of contacting the ship. *Antariksh* was just too far away, and standard radio signals would take years to travel to the ship and back. The scientist in him understood the real problem. While a ship travelling at FTL generated enough power at the local level to shatter the light barrier - a communication signal could be boosted only once - at its source. There was no way enough power could be pumped into a signal, enabling it to cross the light speed barrier in the emptiness of space.

The earliest he now expected to hear from Anara would be when she returned and reached the Oort cloud. There was a signal repeater in that system. Once *Antariksh* came close enough, Anara could use the repeater to transmit signals to Earth. Those signals would bounce off other stations across the solar system before reaching him soon after.

***

As he entered the cabinet room, he couldn't help but feel a little apprehensive for not having anything positive to report. He knew there would not be any recriminations or judgments, but he was the head of the premier space research agency in India. It was his job to keep the communication lines with the spaceship open.

"Good morning, Mr. Prime Minister," he said, while also acknowledging the others in the room. Surprisingly, the defence and home ministers, along with their senior bureaucrats, were also present today. This was unusual if not unexpected.

"Namaste, Sriniji," the Prime Minister answered using the honorific 'Ji'. "Sanjoy was just informing us that there is no fresh information. I know you and your team must be feeling low-spirited - not having any news from your most advanced ship. I have also been praying for the safety of our people."

Srini smiled at the characteristic way the PM understood people and their emotions and made them feel comfortable around him. "You're right as usual, sir. It's disconcerting not to have any news to report. But we're hopeful we'll hear something soon. The journey was supposed to take around eighty weeks, which have now passed. Even giving them enough time to explore the system, I admit, they are overdue from our planned schedule."

"And I'm confident they will be safe and sound. We've given them the best protection possible, and a skilled crew manned the ship itself," said Balraj, the minister of defence. Srini wondered if there was a hint of sarcasm in the minister's voice.

"Anyway, that is not the purpose of today's meeting, Directorji. How is work coming along on *Antariksh-2*?"

Is that what this meeting is about? Good thing I came prepared. Srini called up some charts on the display before speaking. "The project is on schedule, sir. Since we don't have to tackle basic problems like the effect of FTL on humans in space, the timelines are shorter than that for *Antariksh-1*.

We're working on increasing the power available for both propulsion and weapons. That's taking some time to match up with the size of the new vessel."

"I believe that is clear. Go on."

"Well sir, the fact is, if we want to send two hundred people up in space for a journey that can last for many years, we need to equip the ship like a small city. It needs provisions, backup equipment and fuel reserves. That means more resources need to be fit into a ship small enough to be propelled into space at the speed of light. It'll take some more time to work out all the kinks from the design, but I'm confident that we will meet the timelines."

"So, in five years time, we'll have the ship ready to fly?"

"More or less, yes sir."

"Just assume for the moment, Sriniji," said Balraj, "that for the foreseeable future, we only have one ship capable of travelling into interstellar space. Also assume *Antariksh* has run into major trouble at Proxima, and we need to send help. What if unfriendly aliens are on their way to Earth? What will our options be then?"

Srini thought it over before replying. "As you said, sir, with only one interstellar ship, our options are limited. There is nothing else available for us to deploy. The Americans, the French and the Chinese have made considerable progress but will need a few more years before their ships can undergo in-flight testing. We have some short-range vessels available, but we have limited defensive capabilities."

"And if we want to go on the offensive?"

What's on his mind? "Well, sir. With respect, our military will better answer that question. But I believe our offensive capabilities are non-existent."

"What you're saying is that we need at least five years before we can handle any credible threat from outer space?" The PM was pensive. "And what if we decide to replicate *Antariksh* as it is today? How fast can you do it?"

"Well, we have some components available, and it is a proven design," Srini started, pulling up some more data on the display. "If we pull out all the stops and divert people from *Antariksh-2*, I believe I can give you two working vessels in two to three years' time."

"That's better than nothing," said Balraj. "In the meantime, we can equip our current fleet with higher firepower. If not outside the solar system, we can give a bloody nose to anyone who tries a misadventure closer to Earth."

The PM appraised Balraj and then looked up at Srini. "We need both options, Sriniji. I will increase allocations for your department. Sanjoy, get more people on the job. Balraj, can we get some specialists from DRDO?"

As people around the table started taking notes, Srini realized Earth was entering a new era in space - an era of confrontation; not exploration.

"I'll get right to it, sir." Srini nodded.

***

The room below the PMO was off-limits - even to people with the highest security clearance in the country. People from '8' staffed and maintained it.

"This is where we stand," the PM stated as he closed his briefing for the '8'.

"The lack of information is disturbing. My people have reached the same conclusion," said '1' as the rest of the holographic images nodded sagely. "We should work on the premise that the *Antariksh* mission has failed, and we must prepare for the fallout. There are two plausible scenarios. One: The ship has been severely damaged and is now adrift in space with no possibility of return. We may never know what happened to it. That means that we should prepare for a new mission. Or two: they've been captured or destroyed by a hostile alien species, in which case Earth may be in danger."

"If that is the consensus around, then I suggest we get to work preparing for an incursion. To avoid panic and a complete breakdown of law and order we must ensure that the public does not get a whiff of the plans or the potential dangers. Everything will be contained on a need to know basis only," suggested the PM. "Mr. President, you seem distracted. I trust this course of action is acceptable?"

'5' gave a start at being addressed directly. "Yes. Yes, of course. We're in." *I need to get the message out. This is not turning out the way we'd planned.*

5

Three Light-Years From Earth

A second smaller, sleeker shadow was also on its way to Earth. The TrueKif ship had taken off just a few weeks behind *Antariksh* with only eight persons on board - each of them handpicked and fanatically dedicated to the cause. The two pilots on board had been training for a mission like this in secret for many months. Four engineers for maintenance and the two mercenaries made up the rest of the crew.

The ship lacked any creature comforts, made up only of the bridge, engine rooms, and crew rest areas. This was both out of necessity because speed was essential and because they had lacked adequate time to prepare for the mission.

The crew kept to themselves. The pilots could always be found in the bridge or in their rest area just behind it while the engineers kept themselves within the engine rooms, and all of them avoided the mercenaries entirely.

For Jur and Biw, this worked just fine. They had no interest in any interactions. They were living in a different world, trying to learn about Earth from the limited library of information available to them - from the probe and the crew of *Antariksh*. Each played out the scenarios in mind - land on Earth, meet their contact on Earth, get to the destination and carry out the tasks.

Their motivations were as different as their appearance. Jur had been indoctrinated in the TrueKif vision of power and glory at the parent side. As a species of hermaphrodites, all KifrWyss had only one parent. Though they took mates, the concept of a family was limited. Jur's parent had been a senior commander of the Chairman's personal guard. Having earned the Chairman's trust very early, it had become an indispensable personal aide. When the parent retired, the Chairman had shown up at the ceremony personally and taken the young offspring under its wings. The progeny had become a favourite and had been bestowed with increasing responsibilities until the most significant day - being chosen to lead squads on special missions. Unfortunately, the last mission back on HuZryss had ended in disaster, and it was lucky to get a second chance. Failure was not looked at favourably by the Chairman.

Biw, on the other hand, was an enigma even to Jur, keeping aloof even from Jur, unless they trained or worked on a strategy together. It seemed there was an inner fire consuming its very being. There was a hint of madness in the eyes, but mostly there was emptiness. The Chairman had warned Jur about Biw - never trust Biw entirely. And, when the mission is complete, kill Biw too. Once the task had been accomplished, Biw would no longer be needed. But for now,

Biw was a very important pawn in the game. The Chairman needed the commitment Biw brought to the mission.

The military looking TrueKif spaceship raced towards Earth. It had been built for speed, and the skipping between faster-than-light and standard velocity was happening precisely as programmed. This skipping was also having a detrimental effect on the crew's health, but as the Chairman did not expect them to return to KifrWyss, the trade-off between the lives of the crew and speed was acceptable.

Everything and everyone was expendable for the Chairman.

6

Home

Antariksh had finally reached the outer rim of the solar system after a nerve-wracking journey through the Oort cloud. The ship had been designed with three layers of protection against space hazards like dust, rocks, comets, asteroids, and planetesimals. But navigating the cloud at breakneck speeds had stretched the ship to its limits. They were almost at a position from where they could transmit the message of their arrival to Earth along with a coded missive detailing the imminent danger to Earth from the TrueKif.

***

"So, Major, what you're saying is that it is possible that during our exchanges with the Discat, when we handed over maps and other details about Earth, that data may have reached the TrueKif?" Anara was trying one last time to add further information to their meagre understanding of the situation.

"It is a possibility, yes. I'm dead sure they've enough agents and sympathisers among the Discat officials."

"And even then, would it be enough to mount an excursion to Earth?"

"That would be difficult to say. If they want to cause general mayhem, they just need to know where Earth is located. And let's not forget that they might've been able to triangulate the source of the signal that we'd send from GMRT. All in all, they can reach our planet without our help," said Ryan.

"Keep digging, Major. If we can understand the source of their information, we may be able to help Earth pre-empt the strike. In the meantime, we continue transmitting the data we've gathered from the mission and hope they have better luck managing the threat," finished Anara.

***

"It's good to know our ship is safe and coming back home, but how do you plan to tackle this danger?" asked '1'.

"We don't have many options. The information available is just too limited. Even with all the data *Antariksh* has been transmitting to us, we have nothing to take concrete action," replied, '3', the PM.

"I agree. Our analysis suggests that the assets at our disposal across the solar system are pitiful. We have alerted our outposts across the solar system to keep an eye out for any intruders. The only hope is that the alien ship would somehow trigger a warning and they might be thwarted before they reach anywhere near Earth. We have the means at our disposal. Let's deploy them," confirmed '4'.

The resolve of the group visibly strengthened at these words.

"For five decades, the '8' have kept this planet safe from destroying itself. We have eliminated hunger and poverty. We have thwarted terrorists and forestalled wars. With enough power at our disposal, are we not the custodians of peace in the world? Today, the next enormous challenge is in front of us. We will face it, and when the time is right, we will take this battle to the TrueKif's world. We will not give in to fear. Let's get ready for the fight."

***

The initial chaos and alarm had rapidly been replaced with a controlled response as the governments had scrambled to set up an adequate defence.

Meanwhile, the world celebrated the arrival of the spaceship back on Earth. Finding intelligent life elsewhere in the Universe gave new life to the words 'We're not alone'.

Antariksh landed at the MG 1 base on the moon, and the crew was transported to VSSC, Vikram Sarabhai Space Centre, on Earth. The PMO had mandated that portions of the mission were to be classified 'Top Secret' and kept hidden from the general population until the threat from the TrueKif was determined and neutralised. It would be disastrous if it leaked out that humanity's first contact might lead to the destruction of life on Earth. That would be the ultimate irony - life in the Universe was so fragile, and the only two sentient life-forms were now bent on destroying each other.

For the crew, this meant extended medical exams and debriefing. They were sworn to secrecy at the pain of prolonged incarceration in maximum security prisons. Of course, no secret could remain hidden for extended periods, but the expectation was that the crew would keep their trap shut for just a few weeks. Hopefully, by then the bridge would have been crossed.

There were some murmurs of resentment, after all most

of the crew was civilian, but in the end, they all understood the stakes at hand. Some of the team was moved to secure and reasonably comfortable quarters on VSSC.

***

The subject of what to do with the humans from HuZryss had been debated endlessly. The bureaucracy was in favour of moving them to Mumbai to one of the top medical facilities under military care. Anara had fought very hard against this, absolutely determined that Lucy and Joe should remain under the supervision of people known to them till they could better assimilate. She had been consistently overruled but as a slight consolation she had eventually ensured that Dr. Khan would remain their primary physician. It had been emotional for the crew to say goodbye to Lucy and Joe, and they had thrown together an impromptu going away party cum baby shower in the crew lounge just before *Antariksh* landed.

As for the senior crew - Anara, Ryan, and Rawat would go to New Delhi, to join the joint task force that had been formed to pre-empt the expected strike. With no time to rest or acclimatise, the three of them were rushed off to Delhi.

***

Ever since humans had started understanding the nature of the Universe, it had been expected that sometime in the future we would contact alien life. The outcome of this contact was expected to be benign, but many knowledgeable people had been warning about the dangers of reaching out to entirely unknown species. Still, the quest for knowledge would push humankind to take calculated risks in seeking out new life.

Peaceful coexistence was most likely and therefore expected. There had been some contingency planning to handle a full-frontal attack with a massive alien force. The issue, as always, had been to gather enough funding to build a space force capable of defending the planet versus exploring the farthest planets within the solar system. In the end, better judgment had prevailed, and exploration had taken the upper hand. No one had worked on putting together a plan for handling a situation like this, whereby a single marauding ship could threaten the very existence of Earth.

After a few hasty discussions and much fighting over turf, they had decided that the Indian Space Command would handle the search for the alien ship in space, until it was located and destroyed or proven to have landed somewhere on Earth. The IAF would then be tasked to hunt them down within the Earth's atmosphere. In the unlikely scenario, the aliens managed to evade the defences in the sky; things would become decidedly tricky.

Depending on where the landing might take place, the burden would then be on the ground or naval forces. It was likely that the search on the ground would involve multiple groups; hence the NIA was designated the lead agency for India. With their experience in flushing out all violent perpetrators and investigating incidents of terror, they were best suited for the assignment.

All agencies would have an unlimited claim on all resources required for the purpose. The task force would report directly to the Prime Minister and function concurrently out of the control room at VSSC, Thiruvananthapuram and the auxiliary control room at the NIA complex. The two sites had been linked with a virtual holographic connection so that they could function together in real time.

7

Preparations - NIA, New Delhi

For over a hundred years, the NIA or the National Investigation Agency had been the premier criminal investigation agency for India. Within the first few years, it had shown its mettle in handling terrorism-related investigations. Over time it had become the nodal agency tasked with everything from protecting the citizens against terrorism to investigating serious crimes. However, even for NIA veterans, hunting for aliens was something no one could have claimed to have done earlier, though NIA had its fair share of UFO sightings and investigations.

The operations control room at the NIA HQ in New Delhi was the size of an indoor stadium. Giant displays lined up the walls while rows of technicians were busy working at their workstations. One wall directly opposite the entrance was dedicated to the holographic connection with VSCC. For all intents this doubled the size of the enclosed space.

A virtual representation of the solar system was visible in

the centre of the VSCC room. It almost felt as if one could reach across space and touch the planets. Graphics rolled across the display, highlighting all known human-made asset in space. The VSCC was also tapped into every significant space agency across Earth and stations across the system, enabling it to keep tabs on any unexpected visitor.

For all the glory and advanced technology available at hand, the coverage provided was woefully inadequate. There were not more than a couple of dozen ships and stations in active mode connected with Earth, including the farthest one on Pluto. These assets together could not even cover a fraction of the six billion kilometres distance between the Sun and Pluto.

The scientists at ISC were working on the assumption that the best chance of detecting an oncoming spacecraft would be once it entered space closer to Earth, especially after it crossed the orbit of Mars. Most spacecraft and stations were in that general area. Of course, the base stations on Mars would have to be aligned correctly, and the ship would have to pass close by for them to be effective. And then there was another difficulty - that the expected time of arrival was utterly unknown. The brevity of the message from KifrWyss had precluded any possibility of pinpointing the direction of travel. Space was vast after all and three dimensional, the ship could approach from any point. As it was, every scrap of information was being collected, analysed and presented in the control room in real time.

So far, the search had run through the catalogue of all vessels in active status up to Pluto and re-mapped the space debris in Earth and Moon orbits. A secure station in one corner was also tracking classified spacecraft, courtesy of the

'8'. This data was however not shared with anyone - except the AI and the Director of the VSSC.

All weapon systems had been activated and placed on standby, including the Russian laser system on the Moon and the eighteen laser/missile systems in Earth's orbit. These two systems provided the only means of defence for the whole of the planet. At the same time, these were more than a quarter of a century old, and the technology was unlikely to respond to an alien threat in time. The last shield comprised a set of hypersonic planes of the allies, which were kept airborne, flying continuous patrols.

Faced with such uncertainties, more than one leader of the free world cursed themselves for not having shored up the defence of Earth when the opportunity was available. It was now an example of too little too late.

Of course, new ships and defences were being built to protect Earth, but there was no way they could be activated within the next few days and were, therefore, unlikely to be of any help. *Antariksh* was, in fact, the most heavily armed ship in the entire system. However, the headlong dash to get back to Earth had stretched even its vast capabilities. As it lay in the moon dock, repairs and refit were being done on top priority with hundreds of engineers and technicians working on it day and night. If it could be made ready on time, *Antariksh* would probably be the last hope for Earth.

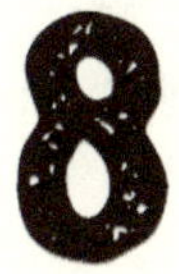

INHS Asvini, Mumbai

Indian Naval Hospital Ship, INHS Asvini, had played the role of the premier research and referral unit of the Indian Navy for hundreds of years. It catered to the whole of the Western Naval Command. The hospital was at the south end of the city of Mumbai in Colaba, overlooking the waters of the Arabian Sea. The buildings were reminiscent of this mega-city's history. Multiple upgrades over the last few decades had ensured that the hospital still fielded top of the line health care for the Indian Navy. Deemed inherently more secure and secluded, this was where Lucy and Joe had been brought.

Lucy's room was completely sterile and bereft of anything except medical instruments. Nurses and doctors in suits and masks were in constant attendance. Since it was expected that her baby would not be carrying immunity to any of Earth's diseases and the mother and her baby could potentially be carriers of any number of unknown pathogens from HuZryss, Lucy had been confined to this room since her return aboard *Antariksh*. She had only caught a few random glimpses of her new home planet during the flight over from VSCC to

Mumbai. The trip on the quadcopter had taken place during the middle of the night, and all she had seen were the lights of a few cities as she sat cocooned in her sterile suit while the craft rapidly took care of the 1700 km distance from T'puram to Mumbai.

A small double-paned window allowed her a limited view of the world outside her room. She had spent many wistful hours staring away at the sea across the rocky shore, just a few hundred meters away. A few fishing and naval vessels were visible in the bay. Lucy could not remember when she had last seen so much water in her life, or such a grey cloud-covered sky.

The continuous babble of voices that floated up to her room even through the sealed windows had fascinated. She felt confined and bored with the inactivity. There had been no further news from her new friends. Fortunately, Dr. Khan always seemed to be at her side. Joe, she had been informed, was in the room next to hers undergoing tests of his own. She hoped they would be reunited soon.

Today, after the completion of her examinations, she was sitting on the bed staring at the screen on the opposite wall. There was some program being displayed on it. The Earth people had called it a 'television' and she had not yet fathomed its purpose. She meant to ask Dr. Khan but there'd always been something else that seemed to be more important. He had told her that the delivery was only a few days away and everything seemed to be normal. She sat up on the bed, feeling restless over the last few days, with a constant dull ache in her back she felt shy in asking for help from the caregivers. The discomfort was mostly bearable, and she had learned to handle it stoically.

She felt another sharp pain in her abdomen. *I hope everything's alright.* The pain disappeared just as quickly as it had erupted. Taking a couple of deep breaths and adjusting her pillows to be more comfortable, her thoughts were interrupted by a couple of beeps from the monitors on the wall. This was the new normal for her and she had learned to tune out the sound.

There was a soft knock on the door, and after a momentary pause, it opened to show the form of Dr. Khan. He was covered in a diaphanous sterile suit from head to toe and was accompanied by a nurse. His face bore the familiar smile he always wore whenever he came to visit her. He entered the room and padded to her side as the airtight door sealed off behind him.

"Hey Lucy, how's the mommy-to-be doing?" he asked standing over her and holding her hand for the briefest of a moment. He turned to check the instrument banks and a small frown crossed his features as the nurse handed him a data pad with the readings over the last few hours.

"Have you been experiencing any pains, Lucy?" he asked.

"Just some aches in my back, but nothing much, Doctor," she replied.

"Are you sure?" he asked again looking at the readings.

"There was a sharp pain in my stomach a little while ago," she ventured. "But it's gone now," she added hastily, lest she causes more concern.

"Hmm, my dear, I think the time is near. That…" he said a little dramatically, "might be the beginning of labour pains. I hope you will handle it. We can still go for a surgery if you change your mind?"

"No!" she said, vehemently shaking her head. "I can cope

with this."

"Okay, it's your call, Lucy," accepted the doctor, while inwardly he admired her determination.

"I have to ask you something," she started tentatively. "Can I go outside and touch the water?" It was a very innocent request, and the doctor wished he could fulfil it.

Instead, he shook his head in regret. "Not just yet. You must stay in quarantine for at least a week after the child's birth. But I promise you; I will show you the wonders of this Earth, starting from this magnificent city of Mumbai. We will ride the old trains, walk along the white sandy beach of Chowpatty and the new underwater city. You can gorge on every type of delicacy this city offers," the doctor said with his eyes shining. "In reasonable quantities of course," he added almost as an afterthought, ever mindful of being a medical man.

"Oh," Lucy's face fell. "How's Joe doing?" she asked, changing the subject.

"He's doing well. Nothing wrong with his appetite or his mood."

"Can I see him? I haven't seen him since we reached this hospital."

"Of course, of course. Just give me a few minutes." The doctor turned on his heels and marched out of the room. He returned a few minutes later leading Joe, who beamed.

Lucy nearly jumped out of bed at Joe and hugged him tight, her distended belly not allowing her to put her arms all around him. He hugged her back with equal intensity. For a short while their world was radiant again.

In the background nurse Aisha did all she could to hide her disgust. This was precisely what RE had warned her about in all their meetings – this was just the first step. Soon other aliens would beguile their way on Earth and take over our beautiful planet.

9

The Arrival

The TrueKif ship was nearing Earth and tension was rising among the crew. The pilot had wanted to use FTL flight almost all the way to Earth, so they could remain undetected for as long as possible, but with the increasing number of interplanetary objects in uncharted space, this would have exponentially increased the risk of collisions. The ship had to fly at cruise speeds only, and that was irritating. They had kept away from planets, moons and asteroids which may have human bases but still the risk of detection rose rapidly at low speeds. The only consolation was that they were less than a day away from Earth and they did have basic navigation charts right up to the landing point.

As the co-pilot monitored the navigation system, identifying and plotting a course for the final leg to Earth, the pilot skilfully manoeuvred the ship to the dark side of the moon. They had been informed that no human bases were present in this area, their ship landed deep inside a crater. They sat tight in that position for a few hours to get some rest. The pilot worked on finalizing the shortest route to their destination. A short flight might give them time to land undetected and give Jur and Biw a few vital minutes.

***

Back on Earth, over the last few days more than a hundred objects had been tracked, investigated and dismissed. The search for the unknown intruder seemed to lead nowhere. There were no reports of any contacts from any of the resources and as an ISC scientist remarked - the solar system was a vast and pretty empty place. With no leads, there was very little to be done except keeping up the vigil.

***

Seven hours later, the TrueKif ship lifted off and turned towards Earth. The pilot had decided to make the last dash for the destination at faster than light speed for less than one second. It had never been done before but it was possible theoretically if the ship's controls responded as designed. It would be perilous over the short distance between the moon and Earth, but they could probably avoid any tracking devices looking for them.

"Radar contact, sir, I have an unknown vessel moving at 100,000 kmph, just entering radar range!" the technician manning the tracking system on MG1 moon outpost called out. Even as his supervisor raced over to his station, the tech called out again. "It's accelerating fast. It's… it's gone. Radar contact lost! I say again, radar contact lost. It was speeding up, and then it just disappeared, sir!"

"They must've accelerated to light speed," cursed the supervisor under his breath. "Get me ISC command immediately and transfer the last known coordinates to them."

***

"Affirm MG 1. Data Received by ISC. Sir, moon base reports an anomalous radar contact. The ship has sped up to light speed towards Earth," the technician at ISC called out.

"Sound the alarm!" responded his supervisor. As the klaxon blared across the two linked command centres, startled technicians and scientists scrambled back to their stations. The atmosphere went from lethargy to chaos in a matter of seconds. The senior supervisor at ISC dropped his cup of coffee and was in front of the tracking map the moment the alarm sounded.

"Do we know their general heading?" he asked.

"No sir, telemetry data is still coming through."

"Copied," the supervisor acknowledged and transferred controls to the next in line–the Indian Air Force, whose team was also embedded in the same control room. "Handing over to IAF control for further action, standing by to support."

"Affirm," replied the IAF supervisor on duty. Then he called out, "Saini sir, handing over command of all assets to you."

Air Commodore Saini, in charge of all air and land assets, did not waste words but simply nodded and instructed his technician. "Alert the hypersonic fleet. Prepare them to engage unknown aircraft. Coordinates to follow."

A series of commands went across to various armed force command modules across Earth. The confirmations came back within seconds. An expectant hush fell over the room while the alarm klaxon continued to blare away in the background.

"Radar contact again. Delayed inputs; high Earth satellite has detected the spacecraft entering Earth's atmosphere, bearing 1-2-0 degrees 1-2-0-0 nautical miles from waypoint

4," the IAF tech called out. As the TrueKif ship rapidly decelerated and entered the atmosphere, there was a large flash.

"Scramble all available assets to those coordinates," commanded Saini. "Give me the estimated time to intercept, for our planes. Quickly!"

"ET twenty-five seconds for USAF 1-3 and thirty-five seconds for IAF 0-7."

"Display map. Overlay expected intercept velocity and coordinates. Let's hope they reach in time."

The primary display immediately changed to show two vectors converging towards the last known position of the TrueKif craft. Velocity and other data crowded the screen.

"It's going to be extremely close," breathed the IAF tech as everyone followed the trajectories of the three crafts.

"We're not being paid to watch, son. Extrapolate the current trajectory and get me the commanders of naval and land tracking assets. This guy seems to have a destination in mind, and we may need to engage him from the ground."

"Speed and bearing unchanged. It's headed right for us."

"Get me the present position!" the Air Commodore nearly screamed at the tech, his patience wearing thin with the needless commentary.

"Yes, sir. Bearing still 1-2-0, 7-5-0 nautical miles."

"This is Air Commodore Saini to commander, Western Naval Command. We have one intruder. Confirm you have it on your radar?"

The reply was immediate, and a hologram-image of the naval commodore appeared. As if on cue, multiple ground assets turned green from red on the central display. The two hyper-craft could be seen steadily reducing the distance to the alien.

***

The pilot of the TrueKif ship was unaware of the ground assets tracking the ship, but it had an excellent idea of the speed of the two ships nearing their position. It did not slacken its own speed but inched the nose slightly upwards, preparing to find a landing position. "Find me a good place to land and hide. As close to our planned coordinates as possible," it barked at the co-pilot. They had lost precious seconds in deceleration and overshot their target.

"It's all forest area, sir," replied the co-pilot, inexperience showing through in the panic of the moment.

"Any large structures where we can hide?" asked the commander while it concentrated on the two ships that would be with them in mere seconds. Their own ship was built for spaceflight; the pilot was unsure how the ship would handle a dogfight in the Earth's atmosphere and gravity. Their first aim would be to avoid a confrontation altogether.

"It's clearing up now. There are some abandoned buildings fifty kilometres from our original destination. I am reading zero power emissions, no signs of life. The structures are large enough to hide us."

"Then punch in the exact coordinates and let's get there." This would take every skill it possessed as a pilot to evade the defenders and land in one piece.

***

The pilot of the USAF Z99 was scanning his instruments on board when he made contact with the TrueKif ship five hundred nautical miles away, which was moving at a tremendous speed. *It seems to be in one mighty hurry,* the pilot thought. His air-to-air missiles and lasers were already armed and only waiting for the signal lock from the on-board computer. That came just a couple of seconds later and six missiles lanced out from the Z99 towards the TrueKif ship.

Every eye in the control room and on the ground followed the missiles as they streaked towards the alien ship. The TrueKif ship was unable or unwilling to take countermeasures and continued steadily on its original path. The missiles gained and raced towards their target.

***

"Six rocket propelled objects following us, range two hundred kilometres and closing. Might be armed!" the co-pilot now shrieked out completely terrified. A growl immediately silenced it.

The pilot concentrated on pushing the craft to the limit as it hurtled down towards the ground. It had to avoid the missiles and still land in one piece, or no one on board would survive the impact at this speed.

Slowly but inexorably the missiles closed in. Air Force control on the ground realised the missiles were facing issues in tracking the ship as two of the missiles exploded a little prematurely. Three others exploded just behind the ship - causing it to rock violently. It was the last one that found its mark just above the engine on the port side. The massive explosion tore the engine apart, and the aircraft tilted to one side. However, the hull of the ship was strong as it was reinforced for FTL space flight and the damage was minimal. With one engine down, the pilot struggled to maintain its approach on the three remaining engines and the ship rapidly lost altitude. The hypersonic aircrafts had to break-off contact as they overflew the alien ship. By the time they turned back, the alien ship had already dipped below their minimum operating altitude.

Meanwhile, the ground tracking radars had picked up the incoming ship and surface-to-air, SAM, missiles now fired from multiple ground launchers.

As the TrueKif pilot reduced the speed of the aircraft to prepare for a landing, it realized the new danger from the ground. The surface-to-air missiles were closing in on the aircraft. In desperation the pilot activated the ship's FTL shields and laser cannons. As the shields engaged the TrueKif ship became invisible to electromagnetic radiation, and the missiles immediately lost track. Safe from the missiles, the ship broke through the monsoon clouds and was lost from view behind the basaltic mountains of the Western Ghats.

***

The people in the control rooms looked at the screen in disbelief as it displayed 'Radar Contact Lost' in bright red letters. With all the technology at their command they'd been unable to shoot down a single craft.

"Excuse me," said Saini somewhat stiffly, his face ashen, "I must brief the Prime Minister. We have failed to prevent the landing, and the search now must continue on the ground. It's all yours now - NIA command."

The entire episode from beginning to end had taken less than ten minutes, and as the men and women came to terms with the situation, they realized the enemy was now at their gate. Its agenda was unknown. The threat was real, and they had lost their only lead.

10

Implications

The parting words of the commodore weighed heavily in the Crisis Management Room at the PMO as those present followed the sequence of events on the holographic display. The ministers, top bureaucrats, and military commanders were too stunned to speak for a moment, and then a babble of voices filled the room as most of them suddenly wanted to offer their opinions and options.

An alert tone from the command phone silenced them. The AI connected the call and Saini faced them on the screen - formally informing them of the failure in neutralising the enemy craft. He started taking personal responsibility for the failure, but the PM waved him off. This was not the time to apportion blame; the man had done his best.

"I need options, gentlemen," the PM asked the gathering in a controlled voice. "Since we don't know the intention of these aliens, we can only conjecture their ultimate destination. They landed near Mumbai, and it may be safe to assume one of our largest and most important cities in the country is now under direct threat of an unknown nature."

"I recommend we get all available military and police personnel on the street, sir. We must get all military assets deployed," offered Balraj. "We will block all entrances and contain them where they have landed while we hunt them down."

"Do you realise that there are thirty million people in that city? Can you even imagine the panic and chaos that will occur when you blockade the city? And just how many soldiers do you intend to put on the streets? A thousand? A million? Even if we managed to gather that many law enforcement officers and automated law and order units, they wouldn't be enough to cover the entire city. Especially not when it becomes known that we have a rogue group of aliens who have landed near the city. If they do not make their intentions known, our people will question; why are they here? Is the public in any danger? The speculations in the media alone will trigger absolute panic. It won't work," stated the home minister blandly.

"Then we must evacuate the city," announced the defence minister firmly.

"Didn't you hear what I just said? There are THIRTY MILLION PEOPLE in the city of Mumbai! How can you possibly hope to evacuate them? And where will you take these people?"

"To top it all, we're in the middle of monsoon season, with half the transport system unable to fly in the weather. Not to mention the Ganesh Chaturthi festival that is taking place as we speak," added his deputy. "Celebrating crowds fill every street corner. Even with all the drones and transports, the surface roads will still be choked with the mammoth processions. It'll be a nightmare navigating the city. Every single officer we have is already on the street. There is no way we can organise a successful evacuation."

"You're convinced that we can't have the military on the streets, we can't evacuate the people and we, of course, have no clue on where the aliens are or how to stop them. Any bright ideas on what we can do instead, besides sitting here twiddling our thumbs?" defence said. He was satisfied to see the deputy turn red in the face.

The Prime Minister raised a hand, and his voice rose above the shouting match, subduing everyone into silence. Quite unlike his usual composed self, he looked genuinely disturbed.

"We have a serious problem, and we also have some of the best people to help us solve it. But, we cannot and must not allow this news to spread. We don't know what the intentions of these aliens are. It's clear that we have two problems to solve, finding these guys and preventing whatever they plan to do. Let's work on concrete actions. Any suggestions?"

"Sir, I respectfully disagree with you," countered defence. "We have confirmed news that these aliens have sneaked in to cause some destruction. That would mean NBC - nuclear, biological or chemical warfare. Look at it this way," he said and called up a display of the city. Concentric circles appeared with their epicentre at Dadar area of the megapolis. "Our smallest nuclear device can flatten an area equal to twenty square kilometres, and it can fit in a suitcase. The worst-case scenario - ten million will die if it explodes in the centre of Mumbai. Even if these guys have a device half that size, we're still looking at five million deaths and an entire city destroyed. This has not happened in the last two hundred years - not since Hiroshima, and we cannot allow it to happen again. And what if they release some chemical agent or a biological virus - how do we prevent those from spreading? We need to evacuate and get our people to safety. That was our original plan."

"I'm well aware of what we had planned for Balraj, but circumstances have changed" retorted the PM sharply. "They are too close to Mumbai. Have you considered the upheaval it will cause if it becomes known that there are alien mercenaries on the loose, possibly carrying the weapons whose destructive power is enormous, as you have just put so eloquently? The entire social order will collapse! We'll be staring at complete anarchy - the city will never recover from it. We will never recover from it politically. I'm also worried that if the aliens detect our attempts to evacuate, they may panic and change their schedule, leaving us with even less time."

The PM got up from his seat and paced around while every eye in the room followed him. "No, evacuation will not work. And don't forget that the xenophobes will have a field day. We've finally found life in the Universe, and even before we can build bridges, our efforts will be in ruins." He shook his head in frustration. "No," he repeated, "we'll never be able to get back into space again. The efforts of centuries will all be in vain. However, if we can capture them, we might still get a chance for a peaceful resolution."

There was silence in the room while people digested the meaning of his words.

"The way I see it, we've only one path left for us - to find and neutralize these aliens. We have some of the best people on the ground. We also have the equipment to back up our teams. Let's use everything at our disposal. Capture them."

The home minister whispered to Tej Kaur, Director General of the NIA, who nodded and spoke up.

"Sir, I understand your concern, and I believe we still have some time to get this done. The aliens may be working to a timetable, or they may be shooting blind. You were right when you said that we don't know what they are planning to do. But it'll be safe to surmise that it involves physical action on the ground. Otherwise, they could've just launched their weapon from the air and escaped by now." She looked around to see if anyone would dispute her reasoning. When no one spoke up, she continued.

"But I believe that they're in a bit of trouble because of their damaged ship. This gives us a window of opportunity. Let's proceed on the assumption that they have landed close to Mumbai for a reason - perhaps because the city is close to where we started sending out signals to their world twenty years ago. And now they need to reach the main city on their own from wherever they have landed. If they have their transport, it'll show up on our traffic monitoring system immediately, and we can neutralise them. If they try to make a run for it on foot, then we must remember that they are the ones on alien terrain. This is our planet and our country, and we know how to defend it." At the end of this long speech, she was happy to see that she had the attention of the entire room.

"What do you suggest we do, Tej?"

"Sir, I propose we run this operation based out of the NIA office in Mumbai. I'll be overseeing the operation. We'll get all available officers into Mumbai and every single military and police asset activated. We know what the aliens look like and we have a rough idea of where they have landed. That's a good place to start. Also, the technical teams can start searching for radiation signatures or unknown chemical agents and viruses. To repeat, our biggest advantage is that we know this planet and these aliens don't. They have no place to hide and no means to reach where they want to go. God willing, I will find them."

The PM contemplated the statement made by Tej Kaur. The show of bravado notwithstanding, he had to agree with the rationale. The aliens were alone on an unknown planet. While they had the element of surprise, they had little else going for them.

"Let's get started then. But please hold on to the plans to get soldiers on the streets. We don't want to cause unnecessary panic and oh, Tej, I suggest you get Anara and her team with you to help. They know the TrueKifs best and may well be able to help you track them down. We'll continue to monitor the situation from here. Other than that - you have a free hand. I'm giving you forty-eight hours to find these aliens and neutralise them. After that - we will evacuate."

Tej acknowledged her orders, her mind racing with the steps she needed to execute.

As some people filed out of the room, the PM pulled the home minister aside. "I may have pushed back the defence minister, but he may be right. I want you to get cracking on drawing up contingency city-wide evacuation plans. We may not have forty-eight hours. And don't tell me it cannot be done. Find a way."

11

Fifty Kilometres from the Mega-City

The dust clouds thrown up by the hard landing had settled - covering it in a shroud and now silence reigned on the TrueKif ship. The pilot's exceptional flying skills had enabled them to land safely. The rear cameras showed their path of entry; deep gouges torn in the building's floor. Inside, the occupants shook off the effects of the impact and slowly got up from their seats to look around.

"Location?" growled the pilot.

"We are at 1-8-N-7-3-E in Earth coordinates, inside some metal and concrete structure, approximately two meters underground," answered the co-pilot as it looked down at the instrument panel. "Atmosphere outside is like KifrWyss, and the ambient moisture level is around 90%. There is no habitation within twenty kilometres and heavy rain. Limited visibility. Feels like home."

"Noted. One of our engines is down, but three are in good working condition. No major structural damage except that the landing struts are finished. We might still be able to take off. Check on the other crew members and report back, while I get the auto-repair robots deployed." The pilot was not pleased with the condition of the ship, but it felt happy that they would still have a fighting chance to fulfil the mission. It had done its part; it was all over to Jur and Biw now.

In the spacecraft's rear, Jur and Biw worked soundlessly, getting ready to start the most challenging part of the mission. Jur set up the transmitter and sent a single coded signal on a wideband. They were supposed to wait for the acknowledgement from their contact on Earth. There was no guarantee of a response, but this provided them with their best chance to navigate to their target through the unknown landscape.

Jur donned the Extra Vehicular Activity, EVA, suit designed for working in alien atmospheres. Of course, they could easily survive in the conditions outside on Earth, as indicated by their instruments. But to have advanced this far and be felled by an unknown biological element was not something they could risk. The suit was completely sealed, providing enough air for seventy-two hours of continuous operation. The auto-deployed armour would stop most projectiles and even survive some hits from laser weapons. The wholly enclosed helmet would provide a heads-up display (HUD) and allow contact with the TrueKif ship, if required.

Jur hefted the heavy Type-4 plasma and projectile weapon and checked whether it was fully charged and loaded. It looked at the rifle lovingly. The two of them had been constant companions for many years. It loved the balance, range and destructive capabilities the weapon provided.

On the other side of the room, Biw sat alone. There was a second suit Biw could use but had decided against using it at least for the time being. *To hell with PiYena and the plans, I am going in raw. I will look these humans in the eye as I extract my revenge.* One side arm for the task would suffice along with the responsibility for the primary device. It was an immense weight on the young shoulders. And then, of course, there was another minor matter to be handled–Biw's personal mission.

Jur turned when the transceiver emitted a sound. It walked up to the transmitter and found their signal had been received and acknowledged. There was another set of coordinates to help them reach the rendezvous point where their ally would meet them. Surprisingly, the Chairman had managed to set up an agent in enemy territory. *It must have something to do with the ship that had landed on HuZryss,* decided Jur, moving it out of mind. *It did not matter how this had been accomplished if it worked.* The preparations were complete.

"Are you ready?" Jur asked.

"Yes. But what is the plan? Now that our ship is damaged, and we don't know where we are exactly. How do we locate the source of the signal - the radio telescope?"

"Nothing changes. The pilot confirmed we are far from the telescope, but we are close to a big city. We will change the target. The city will be better. Let's meet the contact person first. Then we decide. Come now."

The pilot came in just then and nodded at the two mercenaries. It did not grudge the mission assigned to them.

Its own plate was full. Their ship had to be kept hidden from search parties and repaired as soon as possible, sufficiently to fly them off the enemy planet. It watched as Jur and Biw downloaded the ship's coordinates on their own devices, loaded up their gear and moved out exchanging no further words with the crew.

As they left the abandoned building, the engineers set up electromagnetic field emitters to camouflage any emissions from the ship. The ship's drones were already at work, reforming the damage to the ground. In a few minutes, the place would look undisturbed and pristine to anyone who might come to investigate. It would help them stay hidden just a little longer.

***

Jur checked the locational device. They would have to walk at least ten kilometres north-west to reach their rendezvous point, moving through thick jungles. The instrument had detected no human life signs. Night had fallen, and the darkness coupled with heavy rain meant that they could travel without fear of being discovered.

A preset signal was sent again, and they received the acknowledgement along with coordinates. They were supposed to meet at an old railway station, supposedly unused now. Jur did not know what a 'railway' was, but it knew how to read a map. Anyway, help was on the way, and they had two hours to make the distance. Beckoning Biw to keep up, they made their way through the abandoned buildings and overgrown paths. They followed the once wide roads within the complex, through the bushes and weeds, trying to find their way out of the maze of buildings.

Then they came upon a low wall they hoped marked the

boundary of the buildings. Following the wall for some distance, they reached a gate hanging on its hinges. Just beyond it was a river with a narrow bridge spanning it. Staying low and sticking to the sides of the bridge they crossed the river and turned westward, occasionally checking the devices to confirm that they were on the right track.

Jur loved the dark and the feel of the forest made it feel like home. Its vision was well suited to moving at night and it could sense heat from small animals as they scurried out of their path. It walked ahead purposefully, almost in its native element.

Fifteen minutes later, Jur nearly stumbled over a set of metal rails lying on the ground. It felt them with its four hands. The tracks were completely covered with rust and grass, difficult to see in the low light, but Jur turned on its HUD and could make out the rails disappearing in the distance. It checked the direction against its map. Now they only had to follow these tracks to get to Panvel station. They set off at a brisk pace needing little guidance, now that the path was clear. Fortunately, the area was quite deserted, especially at this time of the night. They had been lucky having avoided any signs of civilization. If all went well, they would reach their first destination well in time.

***

The transceiver chirped in his pocket with urgency, but he ignored it. Locating a suitable place to meet the aliens had been relatively easy. A few years back he'd worked near the area the aliens had landed and knew of an abandoned and isolated railway station which would suit their need. The heavy monsoon rains and the dark overcast nights would be his allies.

The overall mission plan had seemed like a great idea when it had been presented to him at first, back at HuZryss. But the months he had spent on the journey back to Earth since that fateful day had nearly convinced him he would not be contacted again. He had been muddled, swinging between hope and fear. Between greed and apprehension. He had almost kissed the promised fortune goodbye. Still, that small glimmer of hope had remained in his heart. It had been reignited by the madcap rush made by *Antariksh* to return to Earth. His fears had been reawakened, and so had his greed. He did not know what role they expected him to play. His brief had been simple - provide all support to whoever reaches out to him from KifrWyss. And don't ask questions.

Getting his act together had been tougher than he'd expected. He had to remain undetected while he went about the task. Fortunately, the medical quarantine on *Antariksh's* return had been lifted quickly, and he'd been able to go back to work while he anxiously waited for the next signal.

He was still not sure how he would explain his absence to his mates, but if all went well, he wouldn't be coming back to this place, ever. He meant to disappear once the job was over. Sri Lanka looked like a good idea to lie low for some time while waiting for things to cool down. Then he'd make his way further south. Fiji would be great for him to disappear permanently.

The details of the mission worried him. He wasn't privy to what the TrueKifs expected to achieve. They had said that it would be a ground operation and he would have to provide logistics and other support. It would, of course, not be easy moving aliens from place to place while keeping them hidden from prying eyes and all the tracking technology employed by law enforcement. That would be a challenge. There were very few private vehicles available, now that shared and public transportation was the norm, and each of these could be tracked easily. He had mulled over this problem for many weeks before deciding that the most straightforward way would also be the safest - he would first take the HyLoop to the city nearest to their landing point and then just hire an autonomous travel pod for the rest of the journey. Hopefully, its anonymity would help hide his visitors. What he was sure was that for all of this to work he would need a lot of money. That was the immediate problem. Lots of untraceable currency.

He pocketed his weapon as he left his room. He wasn't sure it would be needed, but the weight and feel reassured him. After all, this was the tool of his trade. Coming out of the complex, he rapidly made his way down the main road and crossed at a corner. He continued walking for a few hundred meters more. He was not sure how increasing the distance would help him, but it seemed like a good idea.

As he walked, he turned his left wrist over and gestured to bring up his screen. A soft glow told him he was connected to the ComNet, the nationwide communication system. Pressing his finger on the central circle on the screen, he confirmed his identity and first checked if his personal ADID was functional. He then navigated to his finances page, happy to see a healthy balance on his account - the two years in space had earned him a nice sum in back pay. Of course, the authorities could immediately locate him if he used autopay using ADID. He needed to get cash or an anonymous pay card. His first stop would therefore be an old 'friend' who had helped him out once or twice in the past. 'Friend' was stretching it - Karam was like a leech who would suck his blood dry while wishing him a good day. But he was sure that Karam would know all the tricks. Karam would be his first stop.

Flicking his right hand in the air, he waited for a taxi pod to reach his location and take him to the nearest HyLoop line. In less than a minute, an automated pod landed in front of him. As soon as he had settled down in the one-man capsule and entered his destination, he pulled out the minute transceiver and opened it. They had assured him that it would work correctly on Earth and the signal would be untraceable. It seemed to employ some compressed signal packet technology, communicating in bursts while still allowing the two sides to talk normally. He immediately received an answer and was not surprised to hear the person speaking in English. He did not know and did not care whether this was because of automatic translation, or whether they knew the language. Confirming the contact location was unchanged and that he would be there in less than two hours, he shut down the device. He could have turned on the privacy mode on his own ComNet but needed to leave some crumbs for the police to follow. Only then would he switch it off and disappear into the anonymity of a large city. If he disappeared too early, he would be caught just as quickly.

As he sat back in the self-adjusting seat, he closed his eyes and started thinking of all the ways he would spend the loot - no more parades, no more drills and no more officers barking orders at him. In his mind he started off on the design of the villa on his private island, and a satisfied smirk formed on his lips. He silenced the small voice in the back of his mind which wanted to remind him that millions of lives were at stake on his decision.

First Mumbai, then find Karam and finally Panvel. This would be a piece of cake.

12

T Minus 48 Hours - NIA Station, Mumbai

Tejinder Kaur, or Tej as she was better known as, had been appointed Director General of the NIA two years back, holding a three-star rank. Her name meant 'ray of the sun'. It suited her as she was the first daughter born to a family with three sons. She completed her training in 2084 at the Sardar Vallabhbhai Patel National Police Academy in Hyderabad. Originally from the cadre for the northern state of Punjab, she had served in multiple positions in the Indian Police Service before being seconded to the NIA. Her upbringing in a Sikh home, being raised by a father who had been a colonel in the Indian army, and a devout mother, had instilled a sense of fearlessness in her, only somewhat tempered with a calmness born of spirituality.

Today, she had left the PMO chewing over the problem facing her. This was bigger than anything she had ever worked on before, and she knew her swagger had not fooled the PM.

While convinced she could bring this case to a swift conclusion, she knew that time was her enemy. She did not know the schedule these aliens were operating on - it could be days, weeks or even hours. And every minute wasted on trying to locate them brought Mumbai closer to being annihilated.

She hurried out to find her police escort waiting for her. As if things were not bad enough, the PM had insisted she include Anara and her team in the investigation. *Huh!* She needed counter-terrorism experts, not some glorified astronauts who had practically brought the aliens to their doorstep. But the Home Minister had advised her not to push back at this point. "The PM is not in the mood for disagreement," he had said. "Throw them some crumbs and ignore them." She could sense the political machinations in his mind: if the mission failed, they would need scapegoats to take the blame. Anara and the space exploration team would suit the purpose well. So, she had sent word for Anara, Ryan, and Rawat to join her at the HyLoop station. She couldn't cross the PM so early in the mission. Besides, she needed to know everything about the KifrWyss if she was to have any assurance of success. She had already read all the briefing documents from the space mission, but she grudgingly decided she would need first-hand knowledge from the crew.

A couple of minutes later her pod pulled into the city interchange at New Delhi. She saw the crew of *Antariksh* standing by on the HyLoop platform. Without a word, the four of them took their seats and strapped themselves in. The pod sealed shut and, being given priority, it bypassed all waiting pods, and entered the hyper-loop tunnel. It swiftly accelerated to its top speed of over two thousand kilometres per hour. The journey to Mumbai covering a little over fourteen hundred kilometres would take forty-five minutes, giving her enough time to debrief the *Antariksh* team.

"Captain," Tej started off without preamble as the pod reached cruising speed, the walls turned opaque and the gravity management kicked in to shield passengers from the incredible speeds at which they were travelling, "we have very little time. I need you to tell me everything about these… these TrueKif."

Anara nodded and glanced at Ryan sitting opposite her, silently asking him to add to her narrative. "Let me start from the beginning…." she said and did not stop till the end of their journey, sharing the details of the first mission from Earth to the Centauri star system, leaving nothing out. Ryan interjected with his part on handling the attacks in HuZryss space and the strategy he had used in threatening them with nuclear weapons placed on the ships near the human settlement. He explained the KifrWyss did not seem to have thermonuclear weapons, and that tactic had turned the situation around.

Anara suddenly gave a start. "Uh. There might be one thing we should consider." Tej looked at her quizzically. "Do you think they somehow stole the idea of building thermonuclear bombs from us? Do you think that is what they've brought to Earth?"

Tej mulled this thought over. "That sounds plausible, but without getting our hands on them, it would be impossible for us to know for sure. Would they be able to reverse engineer your bomb designs in the short time available?" *I'm stuck with rank amateurs,* she thought, mentally rolling her eyes. *First, they take a bomb into enemy territory, and now they're wondering if the enemy has copied a nuclear weapon within a few days.*

But this tied up well with Tej's scheme. "Nuclear weapons give off radiation, right? We can search for radiation. I've already asked the Nuclear Command Authority to get their teams activated. They will work out of the command centre in Mumbai. That may help us track down the aliens."

"That should help," pitched in Ryan, "except the KifrWyss don't use the same radioactive material like us. They use a couple of other elements to power their ships. So, you may want to scan for additional or unknown radiation or particles."

"Okay. Just let me get the word out to the technical team to get on it. I don't know if they'll be able to do enough, but it's a start."

"I can, of course, get our head engineer Madhavan to join your team. He probably knows more about their technology than anyone else on Earth."

"I think he's still out at VSSC. Let me send a team to pick him up and bring him over to Mumbai." Tej rapidly entered commands on her communicator and spoke at length with her deputy in Mumbai setting up the scan for radiation and getting the chief engineer on board. "Anything else you guys can think of?" she asked, pausing her conversation with Mumbai.

Both Rawat and Ryan shrugged at Anara. She shook her head and spoke to Tej. "Just one other thing. If it's okay with you, we'd like to meet Lucy for a few minutes and see how she's doing."

Becoming sentimental, that too during a counter-terror operation. Anara was behaving like a weepy... "Sure, I'll arrange a visit, but first we need to get to HQ and start the operation."

The HyLoop pod decelerated as it neared its destination

and finally dropped them at Mumbai Central. A waiting escort took them straight to the NIA zonal HQ at Cumballa Hill on Peddar Road.

The old telephone exchange where NIA had started working in Mumbai, a hundred years ago, had been demolished to make way for another glass and steel structure skyscraper. NIA occupied the entire building now, and they ran all investigations for West India out of this office. The roof was covered with antennae and transmitting/receiving equipment that could send communication signals to every corner of Earth.

They entered through the spacious lobby while being automatically scanned for threats. Temporary ID patches for the *Antariksh* crew were handed out, and they were escorted straight to the top floor where the central command area was located. Having worked at ISC and having seen the massive auxiliary control room in Delhi, the three of them were not quite intimidated this time, but the control area was huge by any standards, with scores of techs handling monitoring and tracking screens.

Tej guided them to her office and waved them into comfortable seats across the table. Her senior staff was already assembled, and they immediately launched into tactical analysis and the deployment of forces. Major Rawat and Ryan revelled in the activity, which appealed to them as military commanders and admired the clarity of purpose displayed by the NIA sleuths. Anara soon lost interest in the conversation around her and sat looking out of the wide cwindows at the Arabian Sea. *I wonder how life on Earth was going to change once news of the aliens got out. How much longer could they keep this covert operation under wraps from the public? It would take just one careless mistake for the entire plan to unravel.*

She felt personally responsible for the safety of Lucy, Joe, and the unborn baby. They had come to Earth on her personal guarantee but had then been unceremoniously ushered away into isolation. She also desperately wanted to find out how Lucy was doing. The baby was due any day now. She surreptitiously touched her left wrist and sent a couple of text messages to Dr. Khan. He replied almost immediately, informing her that Lucy was fine and that the baby would, hopefully, be delivered the same day. She looked up to find Tej staring at her intensely and hastily turned off her communicator. She felt like a school child in the presence of the DG even though they were close to each other in age, experience, and rank.

Tej had formed four groups of personnel. One, along with the IAF, would concentrate on searching an area within a hundred-kilometre radius of the last known position of the TrueKif ship. The second would scan for suspicious activity within the city. This was not a simple task under normal conditions and was now even trickier with the annual festival that would culminate in two days. There would be a large movement of local citizens in and out of the city. The third team would work on surveillance of communication signals. The fourth team would work with the country's Nuclear Command Authority or NCA for short, which oversaw all nuclear weapons and responsible for command and control of India's arsenal. They would concentrate on searching for unusual radiation, chemical or biological hazards.

While privacy laws prohibited NIA from listening in to private conversations, for the moment she had been given carte blanche to eavesdrop on any signals her team deemed necessary. The legal implications would be sorted out later. Protocols could and were frequently bypassed by investigators once a specific ability to counter criminals had been developed. Even if the evidence did not stand up in court, no government or police force would allow privacy laws to interfere with investigations. Prevention was primary. Evidence and convictions would follow later. She knew this well, having spent decades in the police force. She firmly believed that privacy had always been and would always remain a myth. The only downside, of course, was getting caught. Then there would be hell to pay.

Having divided the activities among the team, they grabbed cups of tea or coffee and settled down to wait for the break that every investigator expects - the one lead that would set them on track of the perpetrators.

13

T Minus 48 Hours - Stage 1

Panvel station, once a grand edifice, had fallen into obscurity with the advent of HyLoop lines, the township itself now sandwiched between the cities of Mumbai and Pune. Jur and Biw had finally made it to the abandoned building of the old station. It suited them well to remain hidden there till the agent could reach and meet them. At least their contact had responded positively. They were no longer alone on Earth.

The two of them stepped over the railway lines and went to the back of the large building. It was neglected but seemed to be structurally sound and more importantly it was unprotected. Discarding the ground floor in favour of the top levels, they opened the sliding gates and climbed the stairs. Once on the second floor, they settled their loads in one of the empty rooms and carefully secured the door behind them.

Surprisingly, for Jur, the long walk had been exhausting. It must be something to do with higher gravity or the confines of the EVA suit, which was making it difficult to breathe, Jur decided. They probably just needed to rest for some time while they waited. The next few hours or even possibly days were going to be tough, and they needed to exploit every chance to recuperate. Breaking out some rations, they sat quietly chewing on some food packs while occasionally taking sips of water.

Over the last few hours, they had noticed an increase in air traffic in their vicinity, but fortunately, most of the drones and transports were heading east - away from them. They knew that the Earth security forces would be hard at work searching for the downed ship and they would be very vulnerable if they were located. Not knowing what equipment the security forces would use for tracking; both of them had switched on their individual infrared suppressors that they wore on their arms making them effectively invisible to heat sensors and infrared scanners. They were confident that they were secure. For now.

***

The trip into Mumbai on the HyLoop had been uneventful. As he got down at CST Loop terminus, he had decided what he would do. He turned on the privacy mode on his communicator. This would ensure he could not be tracked further from that position onwards. Of course, this was valid provided he did not use his ADID account or use any other electronic services. He had some cash, and that'd have to do till he arranged for single use cards. He checked the local travel boards and stepped on the travellator that would take him to Fort, a short distance away. There in the back alleys behind Flora Fountain, he would locate Karam in his dingy electronics repair shop. He had kept in touch with Karam since his college days and occasionally used him whenever he needed hard cash.

Karam was a small-time dealer in the black market who had his hands in many underhanded deals, ostensibly running a legitimate electronics repair business and so far, avoiding trouble with the law.

He had not informed Karam that he would be dropping in and hoped the dealer would be available. Fortunately, because of his privacy mode, he was not assailed by holographic advertisements and information at every step. It was amazing how intrusive marketing had become. This was one of the few times that he could look at the real world without having to wade through virtual reality.

He located the shop with relative ease, pleased to see the shutter open and the lights on inside. The location in a side street with other nondescript stores afforded ample privacy for what he wanted to achieve. Providentially, there were very few people out on the streets that night. *Most of them must be at home enjoying the long holiday with their families. The monsoon would probably keep other stragglers at bay.* He saw that the weather control system had not been deployed in the area today. That benefited him as the drizzle provided another layer of security.

He stepped up to the door and knocked softly. With the illegal transaction he was about to undertake he would effectively be on the wrong side of the law.

Karam looked up from behind the counter and recognising him, pressed the button to open the door.

Stepping into the shop was like taking a step back in history. The walls were lined with shelves filled with broken down electronics of unknown vintage, and he strongly suspected they could never be made to work again. The proprietor himself resembled his stock of goods - unkempt hair and a worn set of clothes, an unshaven face and shifty eyes.

"Hey man," he greeted Karam with a forced smile to hide his nervousness. He hoped Karam would buy his story facing disciplinary action in the force and needing to disappear for some time. He resisted the urge to wipe perspiration from his face. Fortunately, Karam looked disinterested in the circumstances which had brought him to the shop to seek his services.

"Look, it's not so easy or cheap setting up untraceable transactions, and most places will not accept hard cash, anyway. What you should look for are prepaid cash cards - use and throw. Virtually incapable of being tracked down."

"Just tell me you can help me out, Karam. I don't have much time."

"Yeah. Yeah. Who does nowadays, even for old friends like me?" Karam grinned showing a row of yellowing teeth. "You realise that I don't keep any cards in my shop? It's not safe. I must talk to some people and get them for you. It's too late now. Tell me how much you need and come back in the morning."

"No, no, no…. I can't wait that long. I need two hundred thousand, and I need it now. I'll… I'll double your commission."

Karam peered at him through his glasses across the counter. *Something smells fishy. And where things were suspicious, there was money to be made.* What happened subsequently was none of his business. "Triple and you have a deal. I can do it now, but the risk is much, much higher. Think of my children if I get caught dealing in black money."

"You don't have any children, Karam. Don't try that trick on me." This was going to cost him an arm and a leg. The aliens had better make good on their promise or else he would be completely broke soon. "Okay. Triple. But only if you get me the money within the next fifteen minutes."

"You're in a big hurry, aren't you? Okay. Give me your hand. The guys I deal with need to be paid in advance."

He extended his thumb and Karam pointed it towards his communicator simultaneously entering the amount. The transfer was completed instantaneously, and Karam left him in the shop closing the shutter behind him.

The next fifteen minutes passed in complete silence while he waited sweating. *If this does not work, I might as well go home and forget the fortune. I can't move another step without the money.*

To his relief, exactly fifteen minutes later, Karam opened the shutter and entered, grinning widely. Karam extended the three prepaid cards and watched his old 'friend' grab them and exit his shop without so much a thank you. That did not bother Karam who had plenty of friends like this. He had already been paid, and that's all that mattered. Glancing up to check if the state-of-the-art security camera hidden above a tottering pile of junk video players was still recording, he was pleased to see it working. All well-run businesses needed insurance, and the video was his backup plan.

14

T Minus 48 Hours - INHS Asvini

Dr. Khan looked down on Lucy where she was resting on the bed, being attended to by surgeons and nurses. So far everything seemed in control, and he expected the delivery to be completely normal. The last few days had passed in a blur and he suspected that stress was the cause of the baby coming a few days earlier than expected.

He just wished that Captain Anara would be able to make it to the hospital in time. Lucy had become very attached to her over the last few months; seeing her as a mentor, friend and protector. Anara had also promised to be at Lucy's side for the birth of her baby.

For the moment, there was not much for him to do. He was going to stand aside and let the experts handle his patient. She was still in full quarantine and he was happy there had been no breaches. The Class 1 clean room was holding out well, and he did not expect any further problems in the quarantine for a few more weeks. He was already working on the new regimen to be adopted to develop immunity for the child and mother, which would allow them to live healthy lives on Earth.

For the hundredth time, he glanced at his wrist to see if any further messages had been received from the captain. There was still no word if she would be able to make it. Her last few messages had been very cryptic and brief. He understood she was now extremely busy with the secret operation. He dropped her another line and then left it at that. She would respond whenever possible and there were still a few more hours to go.

There was one more thing he needed to check. "Narada?" tapping his palm, he raised the AI on his communicator. Narada was the name of the AI on the ship, *Antariksh*, available to the crew as a source of information and support.

"Yes, Dr. Khan? I assume you are calling me to check on the progress of your request?"

"Yes, Narada. Have you got anything?"

"I have completed a comparison of Joe and Lucy's DNA with the DNA samples of 1.3 billion people till now. You must appreciate, doctor, that the humans on HuZryss had parents who lived as far back as 140 years. They are all long dead. Their genetic records are not available in any database. With the primitive technology of that period, it is likely their DNA was never collected or analysed. So, we have to fall back on an indirect method, and that is to look for a match in the general population to locate their parents' progeny. This may lead us to their great-grandchildren who might be living today. The percentage of genes that match with the current living blood relatives would be less than 3%. It's like finding a proverbial needle in a haystack. I will give you a better answer when at least 6 billion DNA samples have been compared, 75% of the living population."

"Spare me the math, Narada. Is there any way we can narrow down the search?"

"If we can eliminate some specific genetic or racial types and narrow our geographical parameters, we might move faster."

Dr. Khan thought this through. "We know the human eggs were carried on Voyager, which was launched from the USA. Also, if we only look for matches for Lucy and Joe, then we are looking at people of Caucasian descent possibly living in the USA. Will that help?"

"I have already worked that out, doctor. It will hasten the search, but you must understand that at least five generations have passed till now from 1977. If there is a break of even one step, like a person who did not conceive or if they migrated out of the country, we may miss the match in the reduced sample."

The damned AIs logic was sound as always, but it still did not have the human instinct. The doctor had to trust his guts that this would work.

"Just use those constraints, Narada, narrow your search and let me know as soon as you have found something. The best gift we can give Lucy's child would be to find her family."

15

T Minus 47 Hours - NIA, Mumbai

The level of activity had gone up in the control room over the past hour. The amount of data being fed had increased as the teams had started work on the ground. There had been no fresh developments, and while the NIA teams had been busy executing their specific tasks, the crew members from *Antariksh* were sitting around, busy with their thoughts, feeling out of place.

"Ma'am," a tech called out from the team that was monitoring communications. They watched the DG walk rapidly to the station. Anara followed her. After all, she was part of the investigation team and needed to know if something important was developing.

Tej glanced at her in annoyance but said nothing. *Is she going to keep breathing down my neck? I need to put her in place.*

"What've you found?" Tej asked the technician.

"I am not sure what this means, ma'am, but there've been two signal bursts on this band in the last few minutes," he pointed to a wavy line on his display.

"So?"

"This frequency has not been allocated for civilian use. In fact, it is not used by the police, military, or any other government organization. In all my years of service, I've never seen a signal transmitted this way. If I remember correctly, spy agencies used burst transmissions like these for covert communications, way back in the twentieth century."

Tej thought this over. One anomalous signal may mean nothing, but two in a brief interval, both in burst mode, set off her instincts tingling. "What else do you know?"

"That's all, ma'am. Just the two bursts. No further repetitions."

"Can you locate the source?"

"No, I can't. The bursts were too short, and we're not set up to triangulate this frequency. I can, however, tell you that the two signals originated from different coordinates at least fifty kilometres apart, maybe more. I can, of course, set up location tracking now. It'll take a few minutes, but I can't guarantee results. The signals lasted less than ten microseconds."

"Do it then." She turned to face the technician's supervisor. "I want him off the regular team. Get someone else to man this station and move him to another isolated area. I want 100% non-stop coverage of this frequency. Any more signals and I need to know immediately, and I mean immediately."

"This may be the lead we were looking for," she remarked to her deputy.

"You mean it's an alien signal?"

"Maybe. It's too early to be sure. The question is - who is signalling whom?"

***

Tej returned to her office, sat back in her chair and her eyes became unfocused as she turned the case over in her mind.

It was all conjecture, but she'd learned to trust her instincts, honed over years of police service. *Something was not quite right. The aliens had apparently shown up on Earth to carry out a mission. The mission was most likely to be destructive - that much we know from the transmission sent by RyHiza. This meant that they were likely to select a high-profile target - a place or a person. That much is clear.* Fortunately, the interception of their ship had caused the alien's plan to go awry and given her a glimmer of a chance to prevent whatever misdeed the aliens were planning.

She was sure they could not achieve their aim without enough data on the target. If she likened these aliens to terrorists, they would need information about the goal. It was doubtful that the aliens had visited Earth earlier and given the light years of distances involved, they would not have been able to use Earth's signals to gather information. That only left the data left behind or shared by *Antariksh* during its mission on Proxima or whatever was carried on the probe 'Voyager 1'.

As an intelligence officer, Tej knew, in war or peace, the most important commodity was neither men nor weapons. It was information - knowledge about your enemy and your target. *How many times in history had battles been lost or won because the victor had knowledge of the enemy's plans? The British broke the enigma code machines of the Germans during World War II and gained an unprecedented advantage.* Aldrich Ames also came to her mind, who had worked for the CIA but was a Soviet mole. Similarly, drones in the battlefields of the 21st century had provided invaluable information to the army who could then take down targets with impunity. History was replete with such examples.

However, she doubted the data handed over by *Antariksh* to the KifrWyss would have been adequate to mount an incursion. It required much more than just data when one wanted to infiltrate another world - logistics, transport, detailed maps, communication system and the rest. Only agents on the ground could provide these inputs.

It was becoming clearer now that someone on Earth was helping the aliens. It had to be someone from the crew of *Antariksh.* She left the question hanging. In her mind a thought was forming, its genesis in the 'sleeper cells' used by terrorists and spy agencies of the 20th century during the cold war and the terrorist campaigns. But it puzzled Tej. Sleeper cells took months if not years to activate. The handling agency needed to set up false identities that would withstand detailed scrutiny. That required time, money, and exhaustive long-term planning. But these aliens had never visited Earth. So how would it be possible for them to set up sleeper cells? And if there were no 'sleepers', then who was exchanging messages? It made little sense. If she proceeded on the assumption that the signals were related to the aliens, then there was only one other alternative - there was a turncoat within the system. As farfetched this thought may be, it was the only logical possibility.

Tej set up a secure link with the counter-espionage chief. She was missing something or someone but could not quite put her finger on it. She surveyed the entire room, observing each person as they went about their tasks. Her eyes settled on the three crew members from *Antariksh*, and a light bulb went on in her head.

***

Anara, Ryan, and Rawat sat huddled in the corner of the conference room. Anara was frowning having reached a similar conclusion as the DG. There were enough similarities between the SOS signal received many years ago, which had set off the quest to reach Centauri, and this burst transmission that used an archaic method on an unknown frequency. Her senses were tingling. She was not a trained investigator but years of running operations had taught her to rely on her intuition. She wished Director Srinivas was around so that she could discuss this with him. His tragic death in the moon transport accident a few months back had robbed her of the support of the one person she considered being her biggest mentor and friend. She had not even had time to grieve over the loss.

If her surmise was accurate, it was doubly damning - to her and her crew. The same thought kept running over and over in her mind - *someone on my ship had turned over to the enemy, and I need to find out who.*

***

"How is the search progressing?" asked '5'.

"They are on the job. We need to give them time. They have virtually no leads to go on, but I am confident of their ability," replied '3', the PM.

"Our teams are also standing by to assist, if you require their help," offered '2'.

The PM agreed. "Whichever way the events

play out over the next few days, we must also keep in mind that we may need to go on the offensive."

"What is the latest update on the ship's overhaul?" asked '1'.

"There is extensive work required to be done. I have asked them to expedite repairs and gear up for the next mission at the earliest. The engineers estimate it to take at least four more weeks."

'5' signed off from the meeting, thoughtfully. *That much I have that much time for preparations… Too short to confer with the Chairman. The aliens are on their own for now. Let the NIA locate them first, then I will activate my plan,* he decided.

16

T Minus 46 Hours - Chorbazaar, Mumbai

One problem solved, he made his way to the area known as *chorbazaar*, literally the thieves-market. It was a run-down area, famous as a flea market for many decades. Here one could find antiques, art deco, electronics, stolen items and uniforms of every shape, size, and branch of the government. All available at throwaway prices. He was interested in acquiring the two items - communication sets and camouflage outfits. He remembered his own training - the best place to hide was in plain sight. How this would work with aliens with six limbs was something he would have to work out. Fortunately for him, the chorbazaar came to life only at night, and he could safely shop in the anonymity provided by the semi-darkened streets.

Slowly walking through the narrow, meandering streets, he kept an eye on the stalls while avoiding the scores of human and holographic vendors peddling everything from short eats to local delicacies. The fuel which drove the shoppers and the sellers alike was tea - endless cups of it. People and robots milled about enhancing the look and feel of a flea market. The *chorbazaar* was tolerated by an indulgent government and had been preserved as a heritage site. Even the local police gave it a wide berth.

He noted a couple of stalls that looked promising. One of them had old electronics including a couple of mid-twenty-first century walkie-talkies and the other had coveralls of the type used by oil rig or factory workers.

Just to be on the safe side, he did a couple of circuits of the market to ensure he was not being followed before circling back to the old man with the walkie-talkies. It was relatively easy to pretend to be a collector of communication equipment, and surprisingly he didn't have to bargain hard. Not many people looked for decades-old radios. He used one card to transfer the money and even scored a couple of batteries and chargers for the handsets. Once he put in the batteries, he was pleased that the sets still worked perfectly. The range would be limited but enough for his need. They could discard the alien communication technology. He was just not comfortable with something with which he was not familiar.

His next stop was at the clothes stall where he passed over the bright orange-coloured coveralls for dark-grey boiler suits. He took two of the largest sizes available that he felt would fit the aliens. He also got some boots to go with them. Then he bought a couple of blue helmets to complete the outfit along with a few nose masks cum respirators. He was pleased with his purchase. Clad in the overalls, the extra arms tucked inside, with helmets and masks the aliens could easily pass off as members of a work crew.

He put all the items in a duffel bag and paid off the vendor, while carefully switching off and securing the walkie-talkies. His first card exhausted, he threw it in an open drain and walked off with hurried steps to his next stop. Time was short.

A few blocks away, he reached a row of garages where many travel pods were parked for repairs. Going inside a grubby looking garage, he found a mechanic assembling one pod. A terse negotiation later, money exchanged hands, and he was the proud owner of a travel pod, disconnected from the grid and capable of manual piloting in test mode. It was enough. He was also pleased with his storytelling skills. He had told the mechanic that he was off to a secret meeting with his lover who was married and if the jealous husband found them out, there would be hell to pay. The long-suffering mechanic with five children back at home, sympathised with his situation, while secretly coveting the pleasurable evening awaiting the stranger.

His work in the area done, he got into the pod, threw the duffel at his feet and activated the controls. He also switched off the local piloting guide radar that kept him safe from collisions with the rest of the autonomous networked pods. He needed to pilot this thing manually to avoid detection. Once again, his training would come to his help. If he kept his height below a hundred meters, theoretically he should be able to travel safely. He turned the pod east and settled it into a slow course toward Panvel. Now was not the time to attract attention with undue haste.

***

Fifteen minutes later, he was nearing the location of the aliens. There had, unexpectedly, been a lot of traffic on the way which he suspected was linked to the search for the aliens. He had dutifully kept off the main driveways to minimise chances of running into a search patrol.

Shutting down the engines he landed softly a hundred meters from the railway station. He sat still for five minutes listening for sounds of pursuit or tracking signals before opening the doors and stepping out onto the grass. He pushed the pod under the overhang of a large tree and threw some twigs and branches over it to obscure the shape and carefully walked off towards the station.

He knew that this was the correct location, but he did not know where the aliens would be hiding. *I guess I can risk another burst on the radio to locate the team.* The answer was almost instantaneous as Jur shared the location. He walked the short distance and crossed the rusting rails to climb the derelict building. He looked around carefully for any video or security systems, not that he expected anyone to bother about a deserted place like this. Climbing the two flights of stairs he paused trying to locate the exact room where the aliens waited.

Biw opened a door further down the passageway and beckoned him forward. As he entered the room, it took his eyes some time to adjust to the darkness. Despite his years of military training, he was still taken aback by the appearance of Jur. This guy is packing a punch, he thought, looking at all the gear the alien was carrying.

Well, here I am, and this is how it starts. There is no going back now. He hoped the payment promised for his services would be well worth whatever operation the aliens were planning.

No pleasantries were exchanged, and this was fine with him. Setting his duffel down on the dusty floor he pulled out his purchases. He handed over the overalls first and motioned them to put those on. The aliens first looked at all the gear in front of them and then at each other. They shook their heads and indicated they were just fine with the way they were dressed at the moment. Jur was more comfortable in the body suits with armour and weapons.

He tried to argue the point but gave up in the face of their stubbornness. *I'll have to think of something else. I can't just take them where they want to go while they looked like - well - like aliens.* This was going to be troublesome, he decided, especially looking at Jur who towered head and shoulders above the other two. The Type-4 rifle on its back plus the EVA suit gave it even more bulk.

He would have to find other means as the aliens steadfastly refused to change their appearance. *I don't know what I can do in such this short time.* He glanced over at the rest of the stuff they were carrying and was mystified with the large container kept in the corner of the room. He wondered what that contained, not that it mattered to him.

Next to turn up from his duffel bag were the three walkie-talkies. Military grade with a scrambled frequency even though they were hopelessly outdated. Being old was of no consequence for this mission. They just needed secure communication channels in case they became separated and needed to communicate. He had his ComNet, but the aliens did not. But before they were to proceed any further, he needed to be paid. He decided the taller guy was the leader, but the other person had done all the talking so far.

"Let's get a couple of things right on the table," he started a little apprehensive, hoping his nervousness would not show up in his voice. "I don't care what you guys are up to, but if you need my help, I need to know what you are planning to do.

And… I hope you have my payment."

"I have your payment," started Biw, while slowly getting up from the perch and pacing in front of him, "but how do we know we can trust you?" Biw's command of the language was sufficiently strong now, and Biw hoped the tone conveyed menace - they needed the guy in their control.

Time to play his own games. "You do not," he replied simply. "But seeing that you have no one else on this planet helping you, you don't have any other choice." He fingered the gun in his pocket. Payment be damned, he could just shoot these guys now and take what was rightfully his. But there was the matter of the promise by the Chairman. Money may run out one day but being able to run his own kingdom had its charms. And he was not sure he could take them both down. The armour looked very professional. It was not something his small gun would be able to penetrate.

Jur grunted at this from the corner. When he spoke, his voice was deep and gruff. "Give him payment."

Biw opened a pack, pulled out a pouch and tossed it to the agent who caught it expertly in both hands. He opened it and the contents shined with a flash of brilliance he had never seen before. He pulled out one diamond the size of a large pebble. It had taken some time to make these TrueKifs understand what he wanted in return for the favour he was providing, and it seemed they had brought him exactly what he had asked for. He pulled out a small loupe from his pocket and examined the stone for quality marks about which he had been reading. He was pleased to find it almost flawless. The diamonds would be too hot for Karam to handle; he would have to find other dealers. *Maybe Thailand?*

"Okay, this looks good," he said as he closed the pouch and

put it deep inside his shirt, "Now what are you planning to do?"

Biw pulled out a folded screen from a pocket and spread it on the floor. It came alive with a map of Earth, and a finger pointed out Mumbai.

"We thought we should go to the source of the signal you sent to us many years ago, but your flying crafts spoiled our plans. Jur and I have been talking about modifying our original plan and finding a new target. This is where we want to go," said Biw, emphasizing this by pointing at the city again and expanding the map to enlarge Mumbai and its surroundings.

"The megacity of Mumbai, huh? You sure about this?" Both aliens nodded emphatically.

"Well, that will not be easy, but I'm sure I can work something out," he said with confidence. "If you can tell me what you want to achieve, we can work out the best location."

Biw and Jur exchanged a look, and Jur nodded. For Jur the agent was expendable. Once they got to their destination, he would be eliminated. There was no harm in sharing their objective with him.

"You see that container over there?" Biw pointed to the corner. "That's a *kandaarr,* the most powerful weapon ever made on KifrWyss. We have been working on it in secret for many years. We have refined it based on a weapon design you brought to HuZryss. It is now ready. What better place to test it than on your enemy's lair? We need to get it to the centre of the city. Don't worry - this is just a small prototype for a demonstration. Boom!" he added for dramatic effect. "There will be no more talking, no more space travel to KifrWyss, no more contact! Never again will Earth threaten us!"

17

T Minus 42 Hours - NIA Station

There was a knock on the door, and her deputy entered. Tej nodded at him and he sat down in the chair in front of her.

"Anything new, Abhiram?" she asked.

Superintendent Abhiram, shook his head from across the table. He was as puzzled as anyone else. All the electronic monitoring and human intelligence had turned up nothing so far. Zero. Zilch. *Shunya.*

"What about the signals we had intercepted earlier?"

"They've not been repeated so far, ma'am. We have a dedicated tech keeping a watch. I suspect the aliens have gone underground, possibly busy in preparations."

"I agree. And what's worse is that we don't know the probable target, method or any timelines. This is completely messed up."

"Isn't that why the toughest jobs are handed over to us?"

"Humph," she snorted but nodded in acknowledgement. This was the very reason the NIA was the premier investigative agency in India.

"Let's recap a bit," she said standing up and straightening her dress. For the moment she was wearing a smart blue suit in the official colours. Though warm around the neck, it gave her with freedom of movement and allowed her to carry the communication gear and weapons unobtrusively. She stood in front of the window looking at the skyline of Mumbai. The 'city that never sleeps' seemed to call out to her - so vast and yet so vulnerable.

"We know that an alien ship has landed somewhere nearby this city. The landing point may not have been its original destination since it was shot down by the air force and possibly damaged. If so, the aliens will need time to carry out repairs, and till then, at least the ship is immobile. This probably means that their schedule is probably shot, and this just might play into our hands. The landing area has no potential high-value targets. It is not the seat of the government so we might rule out an attack on VIPs or political figures. That leaves only Mumbai as the new potential target. We've also intercepted some strange signals - which probably are their attempts to establish communication with their agent on Earth. And I believe there is a strong possibility that someone on the crew of *Antariksh* is involved in this."

Abhiram looked up at the last statement in surprise. "You can't be serious ma'am," he blurted out. "They are our heroes. The first humans to travel into interstellar space."

Tej looked at Abhiram blandly. "What does it take to turn a man into a traitor, Abhiram? It is always one of these - radical beliefs, money, sex or blackmail. Every man has a price. While

I don't believe the contact time was enough to convert anyone politically, I am confident that a society similar to Earth would certainly understand the concepts of greed or blackmail."

This logic is sound even if unpalatable. "Do we spy on our own people then?" Abhiram asked. He had done that before, of course, but this was an exceptional case. If it got out that the NIA was keeping tabs on the crew of *Antariksh*, there would be the devil to pay.

"I've already taken care of that. Counterintelligence is on the job carrying out background checks. That won't be so easy, and for them to go any further I need to show CI enough cause without involving the home ministry. And that is where you come in. I'm making you personally responsible for managing Captain Anara. She's going to meet the human female at INHS Asvini. Don't let her out of your sight and report back if you get any leads. For the time being, Anara and her team is not to be included in our core meetings and any information to be shared with them is to be on a need to know basis only." She stared at him. "Find me the mole, Abhiram. Get me my proof."

18

T Minus 42 Hours - Panvel Station

If he had been frightened with the announcement, he chose not to show his fear. He had been expecting something like this ever since that 'Chairman' chap on HuZryss had met him. Now that 'encounter' had been spine-chilling. The Chairman was one scary fellow. It had not taken much time for the Chairman to intimidate, seduce and finally turn him. *There will be many deaths, I'm sure,* he shuddered. *Ignore that. Focus on what needs to be done right now.*

"*Theek hai,*" he instinctively spoke in native Hindi. "Alright. You want to get to Mumbai, and I'll get you there. But what's your objective - your ground zero?" he asked, pointing to the map of the city. "Look here, Mumbai covers over one thousand square kilometres and it's laid out north to south. Technically, it does not have a distinct centre. It's divided into seven basic sectors. This here to the south is SoBo or South Mumbai and to the northeast is Pune. The old industrial belts are in the middle - where we are standing right now. The whole of the island now is a residential area. All business and industrial work areas were relocated many decades ago." He looked up to see Jur and Biw hanging onto his every word.

"*Ab dekho*, if you're looking to send a message to show you're capable of hurting Earth, and you are in India, and not in New York or London, then there are only two places to consider - the Gateway of India, here, or the underwater city, there," he said. He traced his fingers over the Marine Drive and pointed out a spot just beyond it in the Arabian Sea.

The two of them saw a circle, roughly five square kilometres, a few hundred yards away from the Marine Drive.

"That is the underwater city of Shivaji Nagar, just off the coast of Mumbai and home to some fifty thousand people. Exclusive, affluent and inaccessible."

There was another growl from Jur. The voice was deep and sonorous when it spoke. "What is so special about this place?"

"It's the place everyone dreams to live in one day. When the island city became too congested and was running out of living spaces in the 21st century, they shifted all commercial activities out of the current city. It then became an education and residential hub. But the old charm was getting destroyed. So, they built a new city, one that would put to shame the metropolises of old. It stands as an exclusive domain of the rich and powerful. I should imagine that an attack there would shake the nation to its core."

Jur grunted again, and Biw looked at it with disgust. *I must have a chat with him one of these days about grunting all the time.*

"If we decide to attack this underwater city, can you get us there now?"

"No, I can't," he answered simply. Then looking at the expressions on their faces, he added hastily, "Only because we're not ready!"

"Explain," ordered Jur, menacingly raising its four arms.

Words tumbled out of his mouth as he tried to reason. "I've brought only the very basic supplies with me. I did not get any time to prepare. We will need to penetrate an entire city to reach our target, and I can assure you the police force here is the best in the world. Not to mention your stunt with the spacecraft–that will have half the army hunting for us as well. Can you imagine the reaction of the locals when they see heavily armed aliens walking in their midst?"

He waited to see if they believed him and was relieved to see Jur bring down its arms. It and Biw walked aside and whispered to each other.

Biw finally looked back at him. "Do you have another plan?"

He nodded. "Maybe. In two days it is the immersion day for the Ganapati festival. Millions of people will be on the street, and the cops will be busy managing the crowd. The main immersion area is right next to ground zero. That'll be our opportunity to enter unnoticed. We need to keep our heads down for a day, and then I'll get you there." *Gives me time to find out how to dispose of the diamonds as well,* he thought to himself.

"Okay. How much time do you need to prepare?"

"A few hours at least. Can't do much now. It's too late. I'll think of something."

"Okay. Do you also know where they are keeping the humans from HuZryss?" asked Biw, raising the question that had been troubling him for so long.

He was surprised to hear the question. He saw Jur had been startled too but had recovered quickly and continued preparing its rifle.

"I have heard they're being kept in a hospital somewhere in Mumbai. I can probably find out exactly where if you're interested."

"Hmm. Sure. Find out and let me know, okay?" Biw rejoiced inside. If Joe and Lucy were in Mumbai, then the task would be so much easier.

Jur looked up at this, abandoning the pretence of cleaning. "Why do you want to know, Biw?" it asked in a deep voice full of an unspoken threat.

"Nothing special, just curious," Biw replied, trying to be nonchalant. "I was wondering if we would have time to visit them and maybe play a little game. It would be good to pay them back for leaving HuZryss."

Jur grunted, still glowering at Biw. "It is not our plan. No change. Sit down and forget the humans of HuZryss."

Biw shrugged but glanced meaningfully at him - get me the information.

19

T Minus 40 Hours - INHS Asvini

It had been false labour pains. Dr. Khan smiled wanly. *A few more hours of breathing time. She's a strong woman and Joe has been supportive. I wish we had been able to find her blood relatives. That would have been a great gift.* The less than 3% chance Narada had calculated had just been reduced to zero. He cursed himself inwardly.

There was the sound of footsteps in the corridor, and he turned to find Captain Anara walking purposefully towards him. Ryan and Rawat followed close behind her, and they were trailed by two burly Naval MPs and a guy in a blue suit.

"Captain!" he exclaimed, genuinely surprised and pleased to see her.

Anara smiled back at him and compounding the surprise, uncharacteristically hugged him. She felt happy on meeting the stoical doctor after the strain of the last few days. She had been twiddling her thumbs at the NIA HQ anyway, so this was as good a time as any to catch up with Lucy.

"How is my favourite doctor and his favourite patient? I must say, Doctor Khan, you've been completely neglecting your duties to the crew. Here we're sweating it out, hunting aliens while you get to spend time with your adopted family."

The doctor looked visibly flustered till he saw the crooked smile on Ryan's face and realised the captain was only pulling his leg. Relieved, he stepped forward to shake hands all around, even with the young guy in the blue suit, who he learned was with the NIA. Only the two MPs stayed aloof and silent, observing the proceedings from a distance.

Dr. Khan guided them all into his temporary office and offered them tea while bringing them up to date with Lucy's condition.

"I guess you'd like to meet her, am I correct, Captain?" He knew how fond Anara had become of the two humans from HuZryss.

Anara nodded, and he led them out into the corridor, turned left and guided them into the changing room. Only one visitor at a time was allowed inside the quarantine area. Only he and Anara changed into sterile clothing. The others waited in the changing area - observing them through the double panelled windows.

As Anara stepped out of the decontamination chamber into the positive pressure room, Lucy almost jumped up from her bed. Joe, however, reached first and wrapped the captain in a fierce embrace. She could somehow free herself and hug Lucy. The four of them, including the doctor, stood around smiling and tried to talk at the same time. Anara was feeling relieved that she had got the two of them safely across billions of kilometres of space, back to the planet where they belonged.

"How's the mother-to-be doing?" Anara asked playfully.

She was becoming better at interacting with her people, first the doctor and now Lucy. *Ryan would be proud of me,* she thought to herself.

"I am doing well, Captain. The people here are wonderful, and your planet is so beautiful. I just wish I could visit the city," she said looking ruefully at the doctor.

"All in good time, Lucy. Once the child is born, we'll all be waiting to take you around the world. It's your world now too."

As they sat around chatting, the doctor looked at his watch and gestured to the captain. Their visiting time was up, and they needed to go. Heartfelt goodbyes later, the two of them exited into the corridor to find Ryan standing alone, except for the two sentries.

"Where's Rawat?" asked Anara.

"He mentioned something about checking out the security systems. He should be back soon. How're they doing?"

"They seem in good spirits, and we won't have to wait long for the baby. Ah, here's Rawat." They all started walking out. Rawat sidled close and whispered in her ear. She frowned and nodded almost imperceptibly.

"Come, Ryan, I want to show you a few interesting places around this area," she said loud enough for the others to hear.

They exited the hospital through the lobby and walked out under the arched portico. The weather outside was gloomy. This was the monsoon season after all. They had been lucky that the day had been dry so far. They could just see the outline of Oyster Rock in the bay, with its refurbished building that now housed a top-secret monitoring station.

As Ryan proceeded towards their transport to drive them back, Anara held his arm. "Let's take a walk, Ryan. I want to clear my head. I also intend to keep my promise and show you around the area. And it'll be better if we can talk in private."

Leaving the transport behind in the parking lot, the three of them exited the gate of the facility to turn right onto the old Shahid Bhagat Singh Road. It felt good to be back in the open air and feel the moisture-laden breeze from the sea just a few yards away. She, Ryan and Rawat walked ahead while Abhiram trailed behind just out of earshot.

"What's troubling you, Rawat? Why'd you leave Ryan alone at the hospital?" Anara came down straight to business.

"I just went to check the security details at the hospital. I don't like what I see, Captain. For all the noise surrounding the humans of Proxima, the hospital offers minimal security. I'd have never allowed a place and people of such vital importance to be left unprotected like this."

"Maybe it's just their way of avoiding unwanted publicity. The less overt display of security, the better. They must have fast responders around that place. And it is a hospital after all, not an armed naval base."

Rawat shook his head. "That may be so, Captain but I have scouted the place. It is minimally guarded. I don't like it at all. What if the TrueKifs turned up looking for Lucy and Joe? I've asked my commanding officer to help review the security measures. He's promised to see what he can do, but I'm not very hopeful."

"Also," Rawat continued, "this guy, Abhiram, has been dogging our steps ever since we left NIA station. Why do we need to be trailed? Are we not the good guys here? I don't like it at all, Captain," he repeated.

"You are being paranoid. Tej must have sent him along to protect us," countered Ryan.

"Am I being paranoid, Commander? She has not kept us in the loop about the progress in the investigation, right? And tell me, how exactly will one person be able to protect us? Something is going on. Every instinct tells me so."

Anara kept quiet as they walked down the side of the road and entered Colaba market. Once an area chock-full of vehicles and tourists 24 hours a day, it'd been designated vehicle free and had been bereft of traffic for many years now. They turned right, next to the iconic Taj Mahal Hotel and reached the seafront. The majestic frontage of the hotel had not changed over the last century, and the hotel itself was still popular with travellers to Mumbai.

"There might be a reason for all this, Major, but I don't think you will like it," she finally spoke up as they walked straight towards the Gateway of India, dodging sundry tourists and hawkers of trinkets and street food. Some things will never change in India, thought Anara, looking at the surrounding crowds. It felt good to see the activity around her.

"And what might that be, Captain?"

"You heard the discussion about someone on Earth helping the aliens, right? Well, guess what - I think Tej believes that's us."

"What?" exclaimed Ryan and Rawat together.

"Keep your voices down! We don't want to draw unnecessary attention," commanded Anara.

"But that is preposterous! I'm a decorated soldier, and so is Ryan. Surely, there can be no doubt of your allegiance. We did not travel four light-years away from Earth just to be branded as traitors when we return."

Anara laughed mirthlessly. "Traitors may be too strong a word right now. Suspicious would be more like it. That's how the intelligence services work. You of all people should know this, Major. To them, everyone is guilty until proven innocent. Even you must admit - the crew of *Antariksh* is the most likely candidate to help the aliens. No one else has had contact with the TrueKifs except us." She was interrupted by Rawat glancing at his palm as a call came in. He looked at her apologetically, and when she nodded, he moved aside a few steps while his companions waited patiently.

Rawat came back shortly while Abhiram continued to watch the entire scene being played out. "Sorry. That was just someone from the crew checking in. I told him the humans from HuZryss are fine at the naval hospital and so are we. Good to know there are some decent people around still interested in our friends from HuZryss. Anyway, back to the earlier discussion, Captain. If what you said is true and the three of us are under suspicion, then we'd better be on our toes. With your permission, I'd like to make one more call. I want to get someone I trust at the hospital to monitor things. Just in case." He moved ahead a little and spoke to someone and then returned. "Done. Lieutenant Keisham will be here shortly. I've told him to scout out the hospital and try to spend as much time as possible in the general vicinity. Hopefully, he'll not be tailed by the NIA like we are."

"I'm not sure that is a good idea, Major, especially considering the cloud we are under right now, but if you are sure, go ahead."

"You must trust me on this, Captain. I'm doing what's required to keep our friends safe."

They'd reached the Gateway and just stood in front of it, looking out over the sea. Each one was busy with their own thoughts. There were few boats in the water. It was not the fishing season. A few hovercrafts went around their business and tourists milled around.

In just a few hours she had changed from being a hero to being a traitor. It was a sobering prospect.

***

A few yards away, Abhiram turned off his surveillance equipment and put in a call to Tej describing everything he'd seen. To him, it reinforced Tej's analysis, and he told the DG as much.

***

It started to rain, and Ryan summoned their transport. It was time they returned to the NIA office.

20

T Minus 36 Hours – Standstill

The TrueKif ship was completely powered down. Its repairs were going slowly, but the pilot was confident it'd be ready to fly in a few hours. Speed would be slower, and the pilot would need to manage the manoeuvrability of the damaged ship. They had set up a constant watch outside to ensure they remained undetected. Even though there had been several patrol ships scanning the area in the last few hours, the ship was hidden deep inside a building and had remained undetected. The team itself, whenever it ventured out, was careful to mask their heat signatures. Hiding away for another day or two did not look like a problem, and they were under explicit orders not to take unnecessary risks. It had no wish to explore this new planet at all.

***

Tej was getting frustrated with the lack of progress in locating the aliens. She had thrown every bit of technology at her disposal into the hunt, even so, it had not turned up a single clue. *Should I reach out to the commissioner?* With one of the best police forces in the country and access to informants and human intelligence, Mumbai Police might succeed where her team had not. The police would enter the picture eventually anyway, she was sure of that, but she could not admit defeat this early in the game or give up her control of the operation.

Maybe there was another way. An old trick used by intelligence agencies across the world - limited information on a need-to-know-basis. She placed a call to the commissioner to inform him of the current status and seek his help. She would not share all her data right away and she hoped, if nothing else, increased vigilance by the police would make free movement difficult for the aliens. Combined operations would happen when the time was right.

She was aware the PM was briefing the Chief Minister along the same lines. She sat back thinking of her conversation with Abhiram. Things would come to a head with Anara soon. If needed, she was contemplating activating the *Prana* Protocol. Ethics be damned. *I hate traitors.*

***

The night was passing uneventfully. The three of them sat quietly in the darkened room with the windows closed tightly. They had seen several crafts, drones and surface vehicles pass nearby. So far, they had been lucky that no one had approached to investigate the abandoned building itself, but that may change at any moment. For the moment the three of them were sitting in the protective EM environment that masked their body signatures and made them invisible to sensors and tracking equipment.

He was brooding over the next steps he needed to take. He

had to convince these two nut cases to allow him to leave the station building to find safer accommodation. The problem was, they still had half his diamonds.

He rejected plan after plan on how to travel out to their target or even to a safe house. With private ownership of passenger vehicles almost non-existent, he did not have any transport at hand, except for the pod he had travelled in. *I guess it can still be used, but the increased vigilance would mean the chances of getting caught were very high. Public transport may be the only option. Unless…*

He got up excitedly, startling the two mercenaries. Jur reached for the gun and raised it with frightening speed. "Whoa! *Ruko!* Stop!" he almost screamed raising his hands. "I've just got the most brilliant idea. I can get you to the target, and no one will ever suspect a thing, but I need to go to the city to make the arrangements. Don't worry, I'll be back in a few hours, and then we can move out." His eyes shone with his excitement.

"Don't try anything funny," warned Biw.

"I'll be a fool if I try a double cross now. You have what I need. You guys just chill here. I'll be back shortly."

He picked up his empty rucksack and one of the walkie-talkies. "These have a range of almost twenty kilometres. I'll contact you if required. But I suggest radio silence unless absolutely necessary. If I'm not back by 5 p.m., call me."

The two of them looked at him blankly.

"Oh, of course. You have no idea of our time. Here," he said, taking off his digital watch. It was a gift from his father, an old antique and ordinarily, he loathed the idea of parting with it. But now, with his newfound riches, he could buy any number of antique watches he wanted. "I'll set an alarm, so you'll know when it is time." He fiddled with the controls and handed over the watch to Biw. Then with a quick salute, he was out in the corridor closing the door silently behind him, tucking the walkie-talkie in his jacket.

He walked to his pod keeping in the shadows of the trees and stopped a few yards away, looking out for any signs of surveillance. He could hear nothing except the sound of crickets. Satisfied that the pod had not been discovered, he turned on his heels and walked off in the opposite direction. The metro tube station was a kilometre or so away, and he could quickly get an overhead train to the market. The plan firmed up in his mind as he walked, and he was sure it could be managed. He plodded on purposefully, keeping a sharp eye for any disturbances. His combat training kicked in automatically, silently guiding his feet in the still night.

***

Some kilometres away another person was moving equally purposefully to deliver her message. Nurse Aisha had just completed her shift, tending to the aliens in the hospital. The baby was due any day now, and she had to get the word out to her contact. It had taken her all day to gather enough courage for what she planned to do. The head of her local chapter of Radical Earth would know how to use the information she was going to share. Ever since the first contact with aliens, that group had been advocating actively against carrying forward the mission to Alien Centauri. This would be their chance to make a substantial statement.

***

Within the hour, news about aliens in Mumbai had reached the headquarters of RE and its head, Keith. For the last fifteen years, he had been waiting for a chance just like this to make his mark.

Keith turned over the plans in his mind as his assistant stood waiting for instructions.

"Ava, we have waited half a century for this moment. Some call us eco-terrorists and perhaps that is what we are. But now the time is to move ahead from sabotaging oil pipelines." Like many significant movements, violent or otherwise, RE had degenerated into a quasi-military organisation more prone to blackmail than working to protect the environment.

Keith continued speaking, more thinking aloud than speaking to Ava, "In the last few years it has become more difficult to continue our agenda. We need a big bang event to propel RE back in the driving seat. The proposed exploration of the Centauri star system had seemed to be the perfect opportunity to further our cause. But the intense security around the entire mission had meant that RE could not penetrate it. This news of aliens present right here on Earth is a godsend opening. It is time for more direct action."

With the cellular nature of the organisation he headed, no direct links could be established to him. Hence, he was free to go where he pleased without security agencies interfering with his movements. Still, he needed to be careful for a little while longer. One wrong move and it would expose him, possibly facing a very long prison sentence.

He set his assistant to make detailed plans while he flew to Mumbai on the orbital flight. He used the two hours on the plane from New York to firm up his thoughts. Time to do or die before the money dried out.

21

T Minus 32 Hours - ATS

It looked like the time to work with the local police had come earlier than she had expected. Political ramifications and the paucity of time were forcing her hands. Having investigated over two hundred leads sent in by the police and not having uncovered any traces of the aliens, she knew it was time to kick things up a notch and take the next logical step. Her briefing for the commissioner had covered the background and the progress or lack of it. The police may not have the NIA's technical resources, but they had feet on the ground.

Tej was now with the Assistant Commissioner of Police, Shinde, in-charge of the Anti-Terrorism Squad at the Force One headquarters in Goregaon. The ATS of the Mumbai police was a special force set up at the turn of the 21st century to investigate and combat modern day terrorism. It had established a fearsome reputation over the last century, having successfully neutralised several terrorist cells and preventing attacks across the state. Force One was its very own specialised counter-terrorist squad.

The third person at the meeting was a colonel who led the regional unit of the National Security Guard. These elite commandos had been directed to support the NIA to capture the aliens. The chain of command was a bit muddled for Tej's liking, but with the Crisis Management Group at New Delhi calling the shots, there was very little she could do. Anyway, she needed the special forces since the NIA, primarily an investigative agency, lacked offensive capabilities.

She briefed the senior personnel on the threat facing the city and shared whatever little information available to her. A full-scale holographic map of Mumbai was visible on the tactical table between them.

"Let me get this straight, Madam DG - we have an unknown number of aliens on the loose somewhere near the city? We don't know their location, how many of them are on the ground and we don't know what they're planning to achieve?" asked the chief of the ATS. "Is there anything that we do know?"

Tej bit back her sarcastic reply to this jibe. Historically, the ATS and NIA frequently worked on the same cases, and their rivalry was well known. *The chief is right - we don't know squat.*

"That is correct, ACPji," she replied calmly. "We don't have a lot of information and therefore we need to continue maintaining secrecy. We should be prepared to act swiftly once we get credible intelligence. Now here's my plan," she said, bending over the layout. "The local police will have secured most of the public places with security which is highly visible. That will restrict free movement by the aliens. Let's assume the aliens have help on the ground and will try to avoid the general thoroughfares. If I were in their position, I'd be looking for a high-profile target. Also, I assume they know we are in pursuit, so I'd like to accomplish my mission as quickly as I can and get the hell out of here." The surrounding men nodded.

"Therefore, I'd guess we've maybe forty-eight hours on the outside to flush them out. Of course, I only have a little over twenty-four hours left from the deadline the PM has set. But we'll cross that bridge when we get there. I will find them and then it will be up to your forces to take them down. Any thoughts?"

Colonel Sandeep from the NSG stroked his chin. "It's not a question of preparedness, ma'am, but one of resources. I have fifty men with me trained for these types of tactical situations. But they'll not be able to respond fast enough if they're based here at Goregaon. How many people do you have, Chief?"

"I have a hundred and twenty. The rest are already on the ground at strategic locations. I can't recall them."

"That's it? Less than two hundred Special Forces men in all of Mumbai? What about AutoSecs, Chief?" She was referring to the automated police response units.

"We have some of those, but I won't recommend using them in critical situations. They are good for guard duties but just not responsive enough for tactical situations we may encounter. I need humans on the ground." The AutoSecs were getting better, but they were many years from becoming perfect for deployment in special operations. "Let's do it this way. I'll deploy the contingency plan for the city." He gestured, and the map changed to show a system of grids overlaying the infrastructure. Different colours highlighted different areas based on population density and ease of coverage. "We have six core sectors. ATS will take four, and the NSG can take the other two. We get fast response teams located in each sector. That way we cut down our response time once you have a location to zero in." Shinde looked around for confirmation.

"Okay, I can take the south - that's where the naval assets are located, and I have some people on my team from the navy. They should find it easier to integrate. And our second team will be right here in the western suburbs. We can operate out of our HQ." Colonel Sandeep pointed out the areas, and the map changed again to show their deployment.

"Sounds good. Let's get down working on tactics. The information for the teams is that we have a few heavily armed terrorists in the city, okay." the others nodded their agreement. "We'll start deploying within the hour. Alright ma'am, the colonel and I will get back to you once we're in position. But you've got to give us something to run with. I can't get my troops to move without solid intelligence."

Tej acknowledged the truth in his words and turned to go. She could not help them develop their strategy, and she needed to get back to the control room.

22

T Minus 30 Hours - NIA Station

The air-conditioning was effective and kept the temperature comfortable, but Anara was feeling sweaty and trapped in the control room. She adjusted her collar, looking around the people in the room. Wherever she turned to go, Abhiram's eyes seemed to pursue her relentlessly. It was extremely disconcerting. As a senior officer of the ISC, she was not used to such scrutiny.

She and Ryan sat over a screen, listlessly reviewing what they had learned so far. The major had moved off. He seemed to be in constant touch with Keisham, passing on tactical information and instructions. Anara wondered what the DG would think if she discovered Rawat's rogue strategy. She watched as Tej called Abhiram over and closed the door behind him.

***

"What've you got?" asked Tej.

"Counterintelligence reported a short while ago. They've uncovered something during their search of the mission records on *Antariksh*. It seems there was some communication device brought on board. They found traces of two signal bursts while the ship was on HuZryss. The frequency was the same as the ones we discovered earlier."

"Why did we not know about it?"

Abhiram shrugged. "Could be one of two reasons - either the captain was not made aware of this anomaly, or they could have missed it. Or she has deliberately held back this information. Which would mean–"

"–that she is part of the conspiracy."

"It may be far-fetched, ma'am but it's a distinct possibility." Abhiram watched Tej for her reaction, but she turned away. "There's one more thing– it's about the major over there. He's been in constant touch with someone. I can't figure out what exactly he's doing, but he's very cagey about it. Shall I tap his ComNet?"

Tej turned around. "Get CI on it. But only his communications for now. Let's not turn this into a fishing expedition till we have more info."

Abhiram passed on the instructions. The CI promised to get him the details of the conversation being carried out by Rawat within a few minutes. Abhiram activated the view screen. The rear wall transformed, and the NIA logo appeared on it. They waited while the links were accepted, and then transcribed text started flowing across the screen. Counterintelligence had tapped into Rawat's communications and the conversation was being relayed in real time to the room.

"What the…? Is he going ahead with this? Deploying his own men near the naval hospital? Why? Is he setting up a base to support someone else?" said Tej. "This may be a lead. Keep a close eye on him, Abhiram. I'll take care of Captain Anara."

Abhiram nodded and made some quick notes on his pad. *How should I approach this? Is Rawat working for or against the country's interests? What are they up to? My boss is right. We need to put a stop to this duplicity right now.*

***

It was late in the afternoon when Anara finally gave in to the need for a nap and a wash. She went to the NIA safe house to take a quick shower and grab a bite. Ryan went along while the major just shook his head and refused to move from the action centre. He still had a lot to do. Having one person on the ground would not be enough.

As she allowed the warm water to wash out the grime and sweat of the last many hours, Anara allowed her mind to wander. Her position was awkward especially with the intense antipathy Tej felt towards her and her team. She was vacillating between the success of her space mission and the helplessness she was feeling today. It was difficult to watch the action from the side-lines.

She switched on the sonic dryer and ran her fingers through her wet hair. Random thoughts kept running through her mind– Lucy and her baby, *Antariksh* and RyHiza. Once this was over, she would convince her government to send them back to Alpha Centauri with a diplomat. Maybe they could help broker peace between the warring factions. If she escaped the NIA, of course.

She saw her own image in the mirror and examined the dark circles under her eyes. The last few years were taking their toll on her. She couldn't remember the last time she had taken a proper vacation. *I'll go to Kasauli for a few weeks. It will be good to unwind in the silence of the forests away from all this stress. For now, a few hours of nap time sounds so good.*

***

Two hours later, feeling somewhat refreshed, Anara entered the NIA office through the double doors into the lobby and made for the bank of elevators on the left. It surprised her to see the receptionist tense up and one guard raise his hand and speak urgently. She dismissed the thought and pressed her ID to the panel to call an elevator. The panel did not respond, and a small red dot appeared on the top right corner. Frowning, she scanned her patch again, only to find that the panel stayed resolutely silent. Ryan extended his own ID and scanned it. Nothing. They looked at each other in confusion and turned around to find Abhiram standing right behind them.

"I'm sorry Captain, but your access rights have been rescinded."

Anara felt her anger rising at this treatment. "You could've had the courtesy to inform me instead of resorting to this farce," she finally managed through gritted teeth. "On whose authority?"

"That would be mine, Captain," stated Tej, stepping off another elevator that had just arrived. Rawat came out behind her flanked by two security guards.

"The PM specifically asked us to help you out with this investigation. I'm sure he will not be happy to hear about what you are trying to do here."

"The Prime Minister is very well aware of the situation, Anara," retorted Tej, dropping the more formal 'Captain'. "And it so happens that he agrees with my decision. The three of you are to be restricted from access to the ongoing investigation and to be taken into preventive custody."

"Preventive custody?" exclaimed Ryan. "On what charge?"

"High treason and sedition, for starters. Conspiring to help the enemy for seconds and let's not forget threatening the safety of thirty million people."

Anara came face to face with Tej, their noses almost touching. "What the hell do you mean by treason? What are you accusing me of? Helping the aliens?"

Tej did not even bat an eyelid. "That's exactly what I am doing, Anara. I have sufficient evidence to tie you to them. A signalling device has been found on *Antariksh* which is of alien origin and it works on the same frequency that we detected here on Earth." Anara exchanged a look of surprise with Ryan, as Tej continued, "Also, we just found the major setting up his own private covert operation. Right under my nose. Of course, he's refused to make a statement. I can't allow that to happen and you must agree that all of this is very, very suspicious."

Anara gave an exasperated look at the major who stared back defiantly.

"That's your evidence? One signalling device that we obviously knew nothing about, and one covert operation? That's purely circumstantial. You'll be laughed out of court."

"But don't you see, Anara? At this moment I don't need to take you to court. Under the law, the NIA can keep you under preventive security for thirty days, and no court can help you."

Blood drained from Anara's face as she realised what the DG was up to.

"You're making a big mistake, Tej. I know you don't like me, and I know you never wanted us to be in this operation. I don't know what your deputy has been telling you or what else you've turned up against me, but you're making a HUGE mistake!" She punctuated this with a jab to Tej's chest.

"Careful, Anara," warned Tej, keeping her voice level. "You don't want to be hauled in for assault on a public servant." It pleased her to see Anara now turn red in her face. *Serve the traitor right.*

Ryan intervened, "Let it go, Captain. There's nothing more we can do here."

"Wait, Ryan. I'm not done yet. We've nothing to be afraid of. I've travelled to the stars. Handled TrueKifs scum on another planet. This is my home. My country." She pointed her finger at Tej. "Nothing she can do will frighten me. We'll see how you react when people find out that you have arrested the crew of *Antariksh* on a… on a… false charge."

"*False* charge, Anara? Let's just wait and see, shall we? And I'd seriously suggest not going public with this. The people would demand to know the complete story, wouldn't they? What will you tell them? About the threat facing India right now or how thirty million lives are at risk?" Tej replied. "I think not. You might as well go off with your people and leave this job to professionals." She stepped away. "And Captain, if I find so much as a whiff of further interference from you, I'll personally expose your duplicity in the media. I strongly suggest that you stay away from your alien friends. However, I'll give you guys a break. Stay away from this station and the investigation, and I will leave you alone till this is all over. Send them away, Abhiram." The distraction would be out of the way and she could scale down the surveillance on them, focusing on the hunt.

Abhiram and two guards stepped forward, and the trio from *Antariksh* was escorted out of the building.

***

The three of them were left standing perplexed on the sidewalk as their three escorts walked back inside.

"Well, I guess that's that. What do we do now?" Ryan asked as his clothes transformed to become water resistant and protected him from the light rain.

Rawat shrugged as he looked towards Anara. She just stood there shaking with fury and anger at having allowed Tej to get the better of her. "Let's get out of here, find a hotel or something and figure out what to do. No place connected to NIA or ISC, please." She raised her hand to summon a pod while Ryan looked up some options for accommodation.

***

A short while later they entered their assigned suite on the 75th floor of the floating hotel, the only thing Ryan had been able to organize. It was right on Marine Drive, overlooking the Arabian Sea. The spacious lodgings were luxuriously appointed, and the three-room suite offered privacy for everyone.

"Amazing view. I could get used to living like this," remarked Rawat as he scouted the place. "Augmented reality, personal robot chef, climate-controlled balconies, heated indoor pool and our very own artificial intelligence valet. Are you going to put this on our expense account?"

Ryan smiled but did not reply. He settled himself on the sizable three-seater sofa and crossed his legs, waiting for the captain to calm down. She was pacing the living room, fuming. Rawat went to see if he could get some tea, coming back shortly with three steaming cups of green tea, which he placed on the table in the middle of the room.

Rawat was as wound up as the captain but decided this was not the time for him to speak. He went and stood by the window. With a press of a button the window lost its streaming view and turned transparent. It allowed a grand perspective of the sea and dark skies outside. Rawat found it had started raining harder. This would add flavour to the *visarjan,* or idol immersion planned in a day or two, he thought.

"How could she do this to us? That piece of bullshit she told us, wouldn't fool a nursery student. This is personal." Anara finally broke the silence.

The other two were silent for a few moments before Ryan spoke up. "I'm also surprised at the leap of faith these guys have taken though you'd had stated the obvious a few hours back, Captain. But then, I have been expecting this."

"Oh really, Ryan? You've been expecting that we'd be thrown out of the investigation by the NIA chief?"

"Oh, no. No. Not that exactly. But I was expecting something to happen once they worked out the obvious," he replied calmly, sipping from his cup, "however mistaken they may be," he added as an afterthought.

Anara snorted at this and continued her pacing, ignoring her own cup of tea. She could see no way out of this mess. She raised her palm to activate her ComNet but there was only silence. "What now? Are your ComNets working?" she asked, frowning.

Ryan and Rawat tried their communication systems patches and shook their heads in the negative.

"I am connected to the nodes but no response on any channels. I can't connect to the 'net' either," Rawat said, looking at Ryan quizzically.

"Great. She's cut us off from outside contact as well," Anara remarked with vehemence. "What about the hotel systems?"

Rawat asked the suite AI to place an outside call.

"I am sorry, sir but outgoing calls are temporarily not available," answered the AI.

"Why?" Rawat asked.

"I am sorry, but I do not have that information."

"Leave it alone, Major. It looks like the NIA has us well and truly corralled."

"We could always wave a sign for help from the window," observed Ryan with a straight face.

Anara looked at him and burst out laughing. She finally relaxed. Her antipathy for Tej had affected her emotional balance over the last few hours. Deciding to sit down, she chose the chair opposite Ryan and picked up her tea. The warmth of the cup and something about Ryan's demeanour seemed to have a calming effect on her. Rawat pulled himself from admiring the view from the window to join Ryan on the sofa. For a few moments, the three comrades sat in silence, ruminating over their thoughts.

"What do we do now?" Rawat broke the silence. *Damn that NIA woman.* He would never be able to get his hands on the TrueKif.

Anara came out of her reverie, and this time there was a spark in her eyes.

"We go alien hunting, Rawat. But this time on our own."

23

T Minus 28 Hours – Marketplace

He had decided not to stray too far from his base. If he was correct, he should be able to get everything he needed in Panvel city itself. The only danger lay in exposing himself again, but the surrounding crowd reassured him. It would not be too tricky to remain undetected. He was on a quest once more but this time for a fresh set of items. The transport would have to be arranged first. He needed a closed-bodied truck. What he proposed to do was almost insane, but the desperate circumstances require desperate measures.

The truck market was predictably empty of transport vehicles because of the festival. He was thankful that the government had allowed old style electrical trucks to be kept for use by traders. These were used mostly for local transport, especially when carrying consignments by air was too expensive or the distance was too short. He walked over to a middle-aged man sitting in the shade in the truck yard, next to a dark blue truck with a half covered back, emblazoned with

'Saikrupa Carriers' on the side. It would suit him perfectly.

"*Namaste*," he called out. "Is this truck available for hire?"

"*Namaste*," the man acknowledged, taking off his cap and fanning himself slowly with it. "Maybe. Depends on what you need it for. Market *band aahe*. The market is closed today."

"*Nahi. Nahi.* I know the market is shut," he sat down next to the man. "I have a problem. You see, I need to take the idol for immersion tomorrow, but the bloody guy I had hired did not turn up. I'm screwed if I can't find another truck today. So if you can help me…"

"You're not from here," the shrewd eyes appraised him. "Where's the idol?"

"Not far from here. Near old Panvel. I need to go to Mumbai."

"Why Mumbai? The artificial immersion pond is right here," he pointed vaguely to the west.

"I know, but we've always gone to Chowpatty beach. It'll be bad luck to break the tradition," he replied keeping his fingers crossed.

"Aah! *Chaan. Chaan.* Good. But I will drive."

That would be a complication, but I may not have a choice. He did not answer immediately. He peeped into the cabin to see the standard old-fashioned pedals and steering wheel. "We can do that, but what do you say, I take it out for a spin now, and you can bring it over tomorrow? How much for two days?"

A price was quoted, and he bargained with fervour to establish his bona fides. The deal done, he climbed into the truck and started the engine. A bit noisy but that was to be expected of an old vehicle. He drove out of the yard carefully, waving to the man who had gone back to fanning himself.

He drove around the streets looking for his next requirement. After spending an hour, he had still not found a single shop selling idols. He knew it was too late in the festival to buy figurines - especially on the very last day, but there had to be someone looking to dispose of their excess inventory.

Just as he was getting desperate, he spotted a few clay idols by the roadside. They were probably ones that did not get sold this year. He found the person in charge and bought the largest one. He got a couple of street urchins to help him load it onto the back of the truck. As he handed over a few notes as a tip, another idea struck him.

"How would you guys like to earn a bit of extra money tomorrow?" he asked the boys.

"Doing what?" asked the tallest one suspiciously.

"Dancing, of course!" he replied and smiled. "I need a crowd for the *visarjan*. My friends ditched me, and I want to show them I have more than enough people in my group. If you can bring along some more friends, I'll pay you extra." He pulled out a handful of notes, literally his last bit of money and held out his hand.

The boys grabbed at the money, and he gave them directions to meet him just off the old highway later the next morning.

I'm getting good at this cloak and dagger stuff. The next few things would be easy. He needed flowers for the *pooja*, the actual prayer ceremony.

His purchases completed, he set off back to the truck market, driving carefully to avoid attention. He saw increased police presence on the streets, but that was predictable. He reached his destination unmolested and heaved a sigh of relief. Just a few more hours to go. He set about decorating the truck singing a song to Lord Ganesh, while the truck owner watched him from the shadow of the tree, still unhurriedly fanning himself. The extra cash would be most welcome.

24

T Minus 24 Hours - NIA Station

othing! Not one goddamn lead! Twenty-four hours had gone by, and she had nothing to report back to the PMO or the Crisis Management Group. It was like the alien ship and everyone on board had vanished into thin air!

Tej knew, of course, that this was not true. It was most likely that they were hiding, biding their time for whatever malevolent agenda they were contemplating. Her search was closer in form to a jungle 'hunt' than the urban pursuits she was used to. There were no signals for her to intercept, no money trails to unravel, no vehicles to be intercepted and no safe houses to be broken into.

She had not slept for more than a couple of hours in the last two days, and it was affecting her ability to think and plan. She looked through the glass at the control room through bleary eyes. Her team was beginning to show signs of fatigue too. Tea and coffee could only take a person so far. Investigators with hot leads would not get burned out so soon. It was the waiting that killed morale. But she couldn't relax her vigil even for a moment. She had sent Abhiram off for a few hours while the station head stayed back with her. Between the three of them, at least one person needed to have a clear head. Thankfully, she had been informed earlier that the special forces were all in their pre-assigned positions. The commissioner of police had also been briefed on the evacuation plans. At least some parts were working out.

Just one breakthrough is all I need to turn this around, she thought wearily. Where the hell are they hiding? Running through a mental checklist, she searched for anything she might have overlooked. She knew her action on Anara wasn't based on instinct or real evidence but more on the need to show some progress. She may well end up paying for it with her career, but that bridge was to be crossed when she came to it.

For the moment, even the human intelligence and the informant network of the Mumbai Police had not turned up anything. She had been on a call with the commissioner every two hours, till the irritated top cop had rudely told her to shove it. If the NIA could not turn up any fresh information, then there was only so much that feet on the street could achieve. His team was bracing for the oncoming cascade of the *visarjan* and the added complexity of a city-wide evacuation.

The air force search teams had not found any further trace of the alien ship. The area where the ship had landed was a complete mishmash of old abandoned industrial complexes that were now reclaimed by jungles. The forest acted as a buffer zone between the twin cities. A protected forest filled with unknown dangers - not of the four-legged kind but abandoned chemical dumps, leaking radiation traps and many desolate mega structures. Even airborne drones and ships with sophisticated equipment, including magnetometers and ground scanning radars, had been rendered useless.

There were several teams of forest wardens and local police combing the area on foot. But it would take several days, if not weeks, to cover the territory where the ship was most likely to be hiding.

Her last conversation with the PM had been short and unpleasant. For the first time in her life, she was facing the prospect of a major failed mission. Her bravado, so strong just a day before, had not survived the PM's onslaught. Her desperate explanations had fallen on deaf ears. The only silver lining had been her statement that she was close to uncovering the traitor in their midst. While he did not like the fact that Anara had been taken off the operations, he was savvy enough to understand that the political ramifications could always be sorted out later.

She walked listlessly back to her high-backed chair and sat back rubbing her tired eyes. Her determination had not waned, but her body was rebelling against the stress. She sighed and closed her eyes. *Might as well get a bit of shut eye,* she thought to herself. *If I have one more cup of coffee, I'll be bouncing off the walls.*

***

Keith was very pleased with REs progress so far. He had volunteers coming over from all over India and other parts of the world. Their numbers had swelled, and more still were on their way. He needed at least a thousand people to make his stand. He had not yet disclosed the news to the media outlets. The time for that would come soon, but right now he could not afford any leaks. The only complication he could foresee was the festival. It would make the movement of his people difficult, but then again, maybe it would help him instead. The place to hide people was in the middle of even more people. The crowds would be his camouflage.

But his agenda was much bigger than a protest march. Something was going on at the hospital, and he intended to do something about it. Protecting Earth required stronger measures than most governments were willing to employ. Not him. Unencumbered by the need to appease voters and by the process of law, he could take much more drastic actions. His covert team was getting ready in another part of the city. It was a small group, not as well trained as he would have liked but then the time had been too short. He had to make do with whatever he could lay his hands on. At least they were dedicated to him even if only for the money that he offered them.

He believed that getting into the hospital would be relatively easy. He could also easily manage finding the 'new humans'. Escaping with the woman and possibly her child would be trickier. The male was expendable and would be executed on the spot. He would do it himself if his team balked at the prospect. Once he had the mother and baby in his grasp, he would reveal to his followers the danger to society from such aliens. His power, his hold over his followers would grow many-fold, of this, he was certain. Their deaths, in the manner of his choosing and in public, would close this sordid chapter.

He had requisitioned the fastest civilian orbital plane available. It would wait on a ship just off India's maritime boundary, ready to fly in and pick him and his cargo up at a moment's notice.

The preparations were complete. He just hoped his nerves would hold out as he led his rabble to their triumph for all the world to see. He downed his bourbon in a quick gulp and poured another, adding some ice. As he looked across the window to the growing dusk outside, he raised his glass in a mock salute and then drained it again. Another twenty-four hours to glory and tons of money from his backers.

***

Nurse Aisha walked around setting things in place in the hospital room. The baby was due any moment, and the senior doctor had decided to go for a natural birth. The mother was in excellent physical condition, and the scans had revealed no concerns for the baby. The room was being set up for the delivery now, and a neonatal specialist had joined the team. All necessary types of equipment, including a baby incubator, were in place. The room was considerably more crowded than earlier, and Lucy was confined to the bed. She looked bemused at the frenetic activity around the room while holding Joe's hand for comfort.

Dr. Khan stood a little aside in one corner. This was out of his hands now. Battlefield trauma, space sickness, radiation poisoning - he could handle it all, but somehow birthing babies was not his forte. He was happy to leave Lucy in the hands of the extremely competent staff of INHS Asvini. He was more worried that he had been unable to get in touch with the captain ever since she had left the hospital a few hours back. Despite repeatedly trying to get her on the ComNet he did not have any luck. The same was true of Rawat and Ryan. He expected them to be busy looking for the aliens, but he was sure the captain wouldn't want to miss this news. He had left many texts for her and was hoping she would call him back. She could still make it back in time if she wanted to. He wondered if any of the others would know how to get in touch with her. Madhavan was also incommunicado. Maybe Manisha?

The attending surgeon interrupted his train of thoughts. "We're ready. Let's get her in position." Dr. Khan sighed. Captain Anara would have to wait - this was the baby's moment right now. He said a silent prayer and focused on the scene in front of him.

****

The truck was ready and so were all the other preparations. There was nothing more to be accomplished for the day, and he gratefully closed the doors of the truck, having parked it in a dark corner to hide it from pesky eyes. Then he handed over the keys to the owner/driver and wearily trudged back to the station. It had been a very long day, and he was feeling proud of what he'd accomplished alone. He had thoroughly earned the payment.

Reaching the station, he climbed the steps up to the second floor and walked to the room. It was pitch dark inside when he opened the door. He could hear low snoring noises coming from the two occupants. It would be so easy to kill them and take what he wanted, he thought. But this was not the time. His stakes were higher. He wondered why there was no one standing watch. Maybe they're just too tired. They had also forgotten to get in touch with him at 5 p.m.

He didn't know that both TrueKifs were suffering from physical degeneration caused by the multiple jumps on their journey to Earth. The effects had started manifesting themselves, starting with mild headaches and then developing into weakness and nausea.

He entered the room and walked over to the corner where his gear was stored. He arranged the duffel as a headrest, lay down and closed his eyes. A few moments later he too was sound asleep. The EM isolation worked well, insulating the room from all scanning attempts.

Outside, light rain continued to fall while the distant sounds of festivities could be heard in the otherwise quiet night.

25

T Minus 24 Hours - Operation *Moksh*

The scenario planners at the Crisis Management Group had never taken an alien attack into account. The plans for the closest alternative—a devastating terrorist attack or a nuclear strike—were being adapted for the evacuation. Earlier that day, six people had sat in the CMG getting briefed on the likely outcomes of a nuclear attack on any major city of India.

What they had learned from the army general in the last hour had chilled them to the bone. It had been calculated that such a strike would kill five million people within five kilometres of the blast radius. Their deaths would be instantaneous and merciful. At ten kilometres out, casualties would be nearly 50%, progressively decreasing with distance. Ten million would likely be dead within the first few minutes, and fifteen million a month later. It would wipe out half the population and obliterate the city from the face of the Earth.

The entire urban area rendered unfit for habitation for generations to come.

The NIA still had twenty-four hours left of the original deadline issued by the PM. But the preparations for evacuation had to start in case the NIA failed. There was little debate. The order was given and Operation *Moksh*, deliverance, was under way. The CMG prayed silently that the NIA would prevent this catastrophe, but wise men prepare for the eventuality of failure. This was Plan B. The largest ever movement of civilians after the partition of 1947 would take place here in Mumbai, in precisely twenty-four hours. For the general citizens and the media, if they ever got a whiff, this preparation was just a routine military and police exercise to test readiness. This subterfuge would not fool them for any length of time. Panic would have to be managed as well.

The city had been divided into sectors as per a predetermined plan, and sector commanders were moving into position with their troops. At the outskirts of the city, at every army, navy and air force base, swarms of quadcopters, seagoing vessels, tracked vehicles and thousands of soldiers were being assembled from every available army and paramilitary unit. Twelve miles to the west, deep in the Arabian Sea, sailors were receiving their first briefings. Areas of operation were being assigned to each unit commander, and they were passing them on to their NCOs.

The first task would be to secure the borders and stop anyone from entering the danger zone. Four brigades with almost twelve thousand troops and support staff had been tasked for this. There were six destroyers and ten offshore coast guard patrol vessels. The South Western Air command, Pune and Jamnagar stations would secure the skies with hyperplanes, flying continuous sorties at different altitudes. Other air force stations were on standby to render aid as required, ready to fly in at a moment's notice.

Then it would be time for the evacuation itself. Every flying and surface vehicle would be requisitioned and apportioned to various sectors. The emergency override once activated, meant that all private and public autonomous vehicles would come under the control of the central transport computer. No longer capable of going to their destination on their own, the ones carrying passengers would be redirected to the nearest evacuation camp, and then they would proceed to the next collection area to continue the cycle. Managing the two hundred thousand individual vehicles, not counting the larger public transports, would be a headache to be handled by the local traffic police and the army MCOs or Movement Control Officers.

Every commercial plane already in the air would be diverted to a nearby airport once the signal was given. The ones on the ground would be loaded only with passengers and would take off sequentially. These would go to the designated passenger airports away from Mumbai and then wait there.

Even in the best of situations; only twenty-five percent of the population could be moved to safety in the first couple of hours. Evacuations would continue till feasible, but even after six hours of movement, a vast majority would still be in the city at the mercy of the TrueKifs. These would be the casualties of war.

Sixteen emergency shelters were being set up outside the city. These shelters accommodated between two to five hundred thousand casualties. With millions of citizens remaining at risk within the strike zone, all these preparations would not be adequate. There wouldn't be enough hospitals or care workers to handle the victims. Most of the injured would die while waiting for help. There was no workable scenario in which the authorities could protect every unnamed citizen of the megapolis.

Two hundred thousand men and women of the military services started preparing for the longest day of their lives. They were preparing for *vinaash* - annihilation.

26

T Minus 20 Hours - Marine Drive

After the dramatic announcement that they were going alien hunting, Anara, Ryan, and Rawat sat across each other completely unable to come up with any ideas on where and how to begin. Night had fallen and, empty cups of tea/coffee aside, they had nothing to show for their efforts.

At first, they had focused on narrowing down the list of suspects. The table between them was full of names and details of every member of the crew and whatever the three of them could remember of their backgrounds. This, in their opinion, was a list of every potential suspect who could help the aliens here on Earth.

"Maybe we're going about this the wrong way," Rawat suddenly spoke up with a small gleam in his eye. "We'd assumed, no disrespect to the NIA, that the aliens and their agents on Earth need to communicate. And so, we're looking for strange communication signals, right?"

Anara and Ryan kept looking at him, too tired to even nod.

"Right?" Rawat persisted, now getting up and pacing around. His usually immaculate uniform was wrinkled and grimy from the stress of the past two days, but his posture had remained erect. He tried to straighten his shirt and tucked a stray piece back into his trousers.

"Right," the other two finally responded in unison.

"But what if that's a mistake? We should look for silence."

"It's too late in the night for puzzles, Rawat," admonished Ryan quietly. "Why don't you just get to the point?" He poured himself a cup of lukewarm coffee having given up on tea and drank it straight up, hoping that it would clear the cobwebs from his mind.

"We have been looking for strange signals till now. Now assume, just assume, Captain," he added hastily anticipating Anara's response, "that someone on *Antariksh* is responsible for the situation we're in. Isn't it more likely that this individual will isolate himself and would not be communicating with any other person except the aliens? We know that most of the crew members of *Antariksh* have dispersed on extended leaves to their homes. But after the last few years spent working and living together, I'll bet they're all keeping in touch and talking to each other."

The other two were finally alert enough to grasp what the major was implying.

"Go on," encouraged Anara, leaning forward.

"So, the only person who would be guilty is the one keeping quiet. Cut off from everyone and go off on his own."

"This means," started Ryan as realization dawned on him too, "that instead of looking for communication signals, we should look for their absence on our normal ComNet phones. That's brilliant!"

Rawat looked pleased as he sought concurrence from Anara. However, she still looked unconvinced. "It's a good idea, Rawat," she agreed finally. "The only problem is - we've nothing at our disposal to follow up on that lead. We can't just log into the communication systems and take the data. We are isolated too, remember? Communication interception capability is still only with the NIA or the police. And if the NIA has closed the communication option for the rest of the crew, then what?"

"We don't need real-time data, Captain. We can check for the past 48 hours. Additionally, as I understand, however secure any system may seem, it can still be hacked. Mobile networks are just as vulnerable. And… we do have one insider on the NIA team, and another who I affirm is the best all-around hacker outside the National Informatics Centre."

"Who are you talking about?"

"You've forgotten that Madhavan might be the NIA station. He had messaged a few hours earlier that they had asked him to come over. They need him more than us. I'm sure Tej has kept him around otherwise he'd be here with us now. She may not admit it, but she needs his engineering expertise right now and frankly so do we."

"And the hacker you're referring to, wouldn't be Manisha, would it Rawat?" Ryan too had a twinkle in his eye - the caffeine from the coffee had finally kicked in.

Rawat gave him a thumbs-up. "Essentially we have only one problem to solve now. How do we get in touch with Madhavan and Manisha?"

Ryan jumped up excitedly and walked behind the sofa while hitting his head with his hand. "How could I have been so blind? I should still have access to my US military communication system. The NIA does not control that!"

"What are you waiting for then? Get going! Can you connect to Manisha?"

"Not directly, no. But I can connect to Joan, my wife. With the work she'd been doing for the US military, she's connected to the same communications network as I am. Let me see if it still works." He sat back down and rolled up his sleeve. There were three small patches on his skin, just slightly darker. One for the Indian ComNet, a second for ISC and the third was the US military transceiver that he was looking for, buried just below the skin on his left hand.

His triple system was a rarity. Generally, people had one or, at most, two, transceivers implanted by the service providers. Having a third one was uncommon but not unheard of. Since the transceivers drew their power directly from the heat of the human body, they could effectively function indefinitely in sleep mode. There was no need for an external interface since the audio signal could travel to the ears by bone conduction. External interface could be activated as needed only for video. For the people who liked it, signals could also be directly sent to the brain through biological neural interfaces.

He tapped a portion of his skin and was immediately rewarded by an acknowledgment in his ear. "Welcome back, Commander Ryan, how may I help you today?" He smiled at his allies and asked the system to locate and call his wife, Joan.

It took less than a second for the system to respond, finding Joan's details and placing a call. They all waited expectantly for her to answer. Ryan meanwhile interfaced their transceivers locally so that they could all take part in the call. "I'm gonna pay for not being in touch with her, so please disregard the language," he whispered to his confederates.

"Hello?" a sleepy voice finally answered.

"Hey, honey. Sleeping?"

"It's 1 a.m. Ryan! Of course, I'm sleeping!" she replied grumpily. "Where have you been? And why are you calling me at this time of the night? Are you coming home? Is everything all right?" her voice betrayed her concern.

"Everything's fine but I won't be home for some time. We're still in the middle of something. Listen, be an angel and call up Lieutenant Manisha for me, will you?"

"Are you serious, Ryan? You woke me up in the middle of the freaking night to play secretary?"

"Joan," he said soothingly, "it's imperative. Can you connect me, please? I'll explain everything when I get back."

"You'd better," Joan replied, still sounding irritated. "How do I reach her?"

"Just ask for her care of the Indian Air Force and patch me in."

"Ok. Hold on." The line went quiet while Joan connected the call.

Shortly another sleepy voice came into their ears. "Hello? Who's this?"

"Manisha! I'm so glad we got you. Listen, it's me, Ryan and I have the Captain and Major here with me."

"Commander! Captain!" Manisha was suddenly wide awake. "Is something wrong?"

"No, no. Everything's fine, but we need your help. I can't explain right now, Manisha. Come over to this address on the double. Bring your personal computer system. Ask nothing more now, don't talk to anyone and try not to leave any traces. Just get here as fast as you can."

"Of course, sir," she replied dutifully, accepting the odd order like a good trooper. "I'll be there in an hour."

"Hey, soldier!" Joan was back on the line as Rawat and Anara disconnected. "Mind telling me now what this is all about?"

"I'll tell you soon, Joan, as soon as I get back. That's a promise. It's a matter of national security."

"Yeah, yeah, what else is new? Come home soon. Bye."

"Good night, babe," Ryan signed off.

"We're back in business, Captain. I suggest we grab a bit of shut eye till Manisha gets here."

"Might as well, I guess. I do hope she'll get here soon."

"Patience, Captain. Patience. We just need a little more time."

The rain continued to rattle against the windows as the three of them made themselves comfortable on the sofa to catch some sleep.

27

T Minus 18 Hours - INHS Asvini

It had been a long night for the team of doctors even though they were all used to this type of challenging assignments. Lucy had been in labour for over six hours. Her child, it seemed, was refusing to be born naturally. The specialists had been ready to go and deliver with a C-section, but Dr. Khan had prevailed over them to allow nature to take its course.

Finally, late that night, the tension in the room was split by the wailing of the child. They cut the umbilical cord, and the child was taken to be cleaned up and checked by a team of neonatal specialists. Lucy was exhausted from the effort and had sunk in torpor.

After many tests, the girl, all of seven pounds and two ounces, was pronounced wholly healthy and brought over to Lucy for nursing. Dr. Khan stood watching over the merry scene like a proud grandparent which he truly believed himself to be.

Lucy, somewhat lucid now, smiled through her tears looking at her daughter. "I will name her Anara, after the Captain. Do you think she will mind?"

"Of course not, Lucy. I'm sure she'll be delighted. Did you know Anara means passionate wanderer or powerful woman? Both are very descriptive of the Captain and your child. She is after all the daughter of two worlds."

"I only wish her father and the captain were here to see her," said Lucy. "Where is she?" *Was it true? Did she really want him with her now?* Lucy shook her head, driving away memories which seemed distant at that moment.

"She is busy with her duties, but I'm sure she'll be here soon. In the meantime, I want you to rest." He motioned to Nurse Aisha to take the child and put her in the incubator to sleep.

He had tried to project a brave face but inside Dr. Khan was worried. It was unlike the captain not to be present for the birth. He desperately hoped everything was alright. He could not get through to any of the senior staff of *Antariksh* in the last few hours.

28

T Minus 18 Hours - NIA Station

Madhavan sat hunched over his work station. He had been running computer simulations since he'd reached the NIA control room. He had been surprised to have been summoned over and not finding his captain around. Or Ryan. Or Rawat. Superintendent Abhiram was the one who had briefed him on his role, while being evasive about the whereabouts of the crew of *Antariksh*. A little intimidated, Madhavan had gleaned some nuggets of information. The captain seemingly had broken some rules and had been sent out into the field. He was to work alone for all intents and purposes, valued for his capability, but not completely trusted for his allegiance to Anara.

The engineer was trying to figure out the ionizing radiation he expected the alien vessel to be giving off. With access to the database on *Antariksh* and connection to Narada, he felt he was making some progress. He was now programming the detectors placed across the city and on the search ships so that the probe for the radiation sources could start in earnest.

It was much more difficult for him to work alone. He had become used to leading a team of engineers and had forgotten a lot of the programming required. If only Manisha were here. She would have done this in a jiffy. The girl is a genius with computer systems.

Madhavan had been pointedly ignoring the murmurs among the technicians - the abruptly stopped conversations, the sideways glances and Abhiram silently standing behind him. He had tried speaking to the DG but had been stonewalled by Abhiram, leaving him with several questions and no answers.

There was a small buzz, and a voice spoke in his ear. "Incoming call from Manisha. Answer or ignore." Deciding to be cautious, he diverted the call to text and opened a window on his screen.

"Manisha, what a surprise! I was just thinking about you," he typed.

"Good to talk to you too, sir. Are you alone now?"

He glanced around quickly. Everyone seemed to ignore him. "Yes. We're good. What's up?"

"Sorry, sir. No time for chit chat. I'm sending you some instructions. You need to connect me to the NIA computer system. I'll take over from there."

"You want me to help you hack the NIA? What the hell is wrong with you?"

"Not hack, sir. Just borrow. Captain's orders."

"Captain's orders? Is she there with you? Man, I've been getting some weird vibes here. Is she all right?"

"We're all fine, sir. The setup please?" Manisha was trying to be patient, but the captain was breathing down her neck, and she knew Anara was desperate to get going.

"Ok. Ok. Hold on."

***

"Is he doing it?" asked Anara.

"Yes, ma'am. It'll take a minute for the files to get installed."

"Where did you learn to do this?" Ryan asked, impressed by her skills.

"Self-taught ethical hacker, sir. Three times university champion. This was also a required course for my communications training with the air force. Of course, the art has developed considerably from a hundred years ago. But it is still humans against computers." Her pride was unmistakable, and Anara couldn't help smiling. She patted Manisha on the back.

"Will the NIA be able to find us out? Will you be able to hack their system? I thought it'd be invulnerable."

"With all respect, Captain, no system is completely fool proof. There are always loopholes. It just takes time to locate them. Additionally, the system AI's will also be engaged to look for evolving threats. However, in this case, I realise your urgency. So, instead of hacking the NIA system, I am just 'borrowing' it."

Everyone looked at her quizzically, and Manisha realised she needed to explain further. "I believe the ComNet service providers have weaker system security. So, I'm going to ride on the NIA network and route a request to the ComNet server and fool it into giving me the information I need."

This girl is going places, thought Anara as she looked approvingly at the petite figure sitting in front of her virtual keyboard. "And you still prefer a keyboard instead of using a neural interface? Won't a direct brain connection be faster?"

"Never trusted neural interfaces, ma'am. You never know what else it might pick up from my mind. Keyboards are less obtrusive and more private. Besides, I enjoy working on a keyboard," Manisha answered with a smile.

"And we're ready," she announced as her screen showed the NIA logo. She rapidly entered a series of complex commands and started responding to various inputs her system was providing. Her concentration was complete, and the other three backed off to give her space.

"I knew she was good, but this is genius level work, Ryan," commented Anara.

"I know. That's why I thought of her first."

"Can someone get me a cup of coffee?" Manisha called out. Then, suddenly realising who she was addressing, she added "Please," a little sheepishly.

"It's all right. I'll get you a cup," Rawat said as he moved towards the kitchen, "and I'll see if I can order something to eat too. I don't know about you, but I'm famished."

***

An hour later, Manisha was still working on her system while the rest lounged around waiting for her to complete the task.

"I'm in," she declared suddenly. A final tap and the screen showed the logo of the ComNet. "Where do you want me to start, Captain?" she asked with a sparkle in her eyes.

"That's incredible! Manisha. Ok, let's see, we need to download the call records for all the personnel who were aboard *Antariksh*. After that, we need to look for aberrations - specifically people who have not been using the ComNet at all. Let's keep the date range for the last two weeks, starting with the day we landed."

"Sure. I can get the list of people from *Antariksh's* computer, but it'll take some time to download all the records."

"Then we'd better start immediately, hadn't we?"

Manisha uploaded fifty-five names and waited for the reply. A long series of names, numbers, dates and times scrolled across the screen.

"Our guys sure have been busy," Rawat smirked as he looked at the screen. "That's a lot of data. How do we analyse it?"

Anara had been expecting the hacking to be difficult but apparently so was data analysis.

"Well, since you're looking for people who have made very few calls, I can sort these into the number of calls made per person." Manisha's fingers input the commands on the virtual keyboard. The system would have readily accepted voice inputs from her, but she still preferred the two-part keyboard.

A fresh set of data resolved itself on the screen. "This is it. All listed from low to high."

Anara thought it over once more, and then instructed, "Narrow down the date range, Manisha. Start from the time the alien ship landed on Earth."

Manisha selected a section of the data and displayed a new set of numbers and names. There were five on the top of the list who had practically not used the ComNet at all.

The very first name was Dr. Khan.

"Rafiq? I don't believe it!" exclaimed Anara.

"Hold on, Captain. Let's not jump to conclusions," said Ryan. "He's been at the hospital the whole time. He would not have been able to call anyone. He probably could not use the ComNet in the sterile room at all. And he had made calls to you. Look here."

Anara relaxed as she received this confirmation. The next three names were hers, Ryan's and Rawat's but she could not quite place the last name - Nish.

But Rawat recognised him. "What the… Of course! Why didn't I think of it earlier?"

"I recall that name, Rawat. Wasn't he one of your security people who went down to HuZryss with us?"

"Yes, Captain. He was on the surface with us."

"That's right. I remember it too. He was one of the security personnel. But how do you think he got turned?" added Ryan.

Rawat paced around as he tried to piece everything together in his mind. "I can only guess what could've happened. You remember, when the TrueKifs were landing I dispersed the security team and asked them to hide? Nish was one of them. We did not contact him again till he met Lieutenant Keisham while he was placing the bomb on the TrueKif ship. That means Nish was missing for almost a day. Those TrueKifs must have gotten to him then." Rawat looked as Anara absorbed this information. "I mean it is conjecture, of course, but the possibility is strong based on circumstantial evidence. I don't know what inducement they would have used on Nish - threats, money?" He shrugged. "They're even more cunning than I realised. It's all my fault."

"I don't see how you could've prevented this from happening, Rawat. Anyway, the important thing is - what do we do now? Can we locate him using his ComNet signal, Manisha?"

"I'll try, Captain," she acknowledged as she bent over her keyboard. "He's not showing up on the system. It looks like he's turned on the privacy function. Sorry."

"That definitely implicates him in my books!" declared

Rawat with finality.

"Let's not jump to conclusions so fast. Just because he has not been communicating does not make him a traitor," offered Ryan. "We can't just condemn a man on one piece of evidence. I think we should get to Tej with this info, Captain."

"I'm not going back to that… that…," Anara lost control. "Certainly not after she's burnt me." *This is not me. I must approach this calmly. Tej had her reasons. Tej could not afford making any mistakes, not with three million lives at stake. Besides she's the most competent person to act on this information.*

"Captain, we need to be reasonable here," Ryan said. "She and the NIA are the only ones who can search for him if he's the perpetrator and is off the grid. There's much more at stake than your hurt ego. This may be the very lead the NIA has been looking for."

This deflated Anara a bit more. *Am I petty?*

"You may be right, but I just can't bring myself to go back to NIA. All right, we will try to meet her, but you do the talking this time. I'm not sure I can keep my cool. Manisha, you can stay here. Try to get some sleep. I'll call you if I need you again and that was a damn fine piece of work." She was not surprised to see the young girl blush at this praise.

"Lead us on, Rawat. This was your idea after all."

Dawn was just breaking over the sea, bringing a tinge of red to the overcast sky.

29

T Minus 12 Hours - Panvel Station

Biw woke up with a start. *Damn, did I sleep through the night? This was not good.* They had lost sight of their objective, even if only temporarily. Good thing the Chairman was not here to see them sleeping in the derelict building instead of diligently working to fulfil their purpose. They would have lost their heads by now. Rolling over and giving a considerable nudge to Jur, he was rewarded with a grunt and a curse.

Jur sat up too, blinking its eyes, just as surprised as Biw to find itself in this position. They looked over to see the Nish sleeping; spread out in the corner, snoring lightly.

Ignoring him for the moment, they gathered their weapons and got ready for the day. Still not very clear on the actual plan, they knew that their success depended on the traitor peacefully sleeping in the room.

Finally, unwilling to wait any longer, Jur went over and kicked Nish in the back. This made Nish cry out. He sat up and looked at the two mercenaries in irritation. His dream of ruling a kingdom had been rudely interrupted. He got up, nodded curtly and collected his own weapon and took a sip of water.

"So, what's the plan?" asked Biw, now impatient to get on with the job. Once that part was finished, another matter needed to be taken care of - the real task.

Nish stretched and wished he could get a cup of tea. However, these two barbarians would not understand the importance of the morning cuppa, he thought. So instead he reconciled himself to sipping some more water and taking a bite from a nutritional bar from his backpack.

He outlined the plan succinctly. The truck was ready and decked up to carry the idol. It would be with them shortly. Amid hundreds of vehicles making their way into the city for the immersion, their anonymity was guaranteed. He would sit with the driver in front while Biw and Jur would be in the back of the truck. Nish had a brilliant if not insane idea to hide them in plain sight. The two aliens would be mythical demons being crushed by God. This was a recurring theme in Hindu festivals - the end of tyranny through the generous and courageous act of a god. That would be the theme for his idol too.

He hoped no one would pay closer attention to the two demon figures lying supine at the bottom of the truck covered in flowers and various offerings. To any inquisitive eye, he would explain them as masterful copies made by unknown craftsmen. Even in daylight, they looked formidable; at night, they'd be frightening.

Jur and Biw did not know what he was talking about but as they had no other alternative, they had to stick with whatever wild idea Nish had dreamt up.

They would need a few hours to navigate through the crowded streets. The truck would not move faster than a few miles an hour once it entered the main thoroughfare for the immersion. There would be plenty of music and dancing going around, and the festivities would be a sight to watch. Too bad it would all end in mayhem before the night was over.

They would take the main Mumbai-Pune Highway before turning into the old Eastern Express Highway. Then onto the suburb of Sion, cross over to the western part of the city and continue onwards to Chowpatty beach. He would have to time everything carefully. Too early and they would be sitting at the beachside being harangued by the cops to move the truck and make way for the others. Too late and they would never get to the beach, being crowded out by the mega idols on the way to immersion.

Once at Chowpatty, he and his young helpers would carry the idol and the demons on a hover-cart to the sea. They would be one among many devotees standing waist deep in the water - watching the idol being claimed by the waves. The aliens would use this opportunity to slip into the water. Once undersea, Jur and Biw would swim out to the underwater city and find their way inside. Nish did not have an exact route into the underwater city yet, but he was pretty sure they could use one of the maintenance ports. Once the aliens were inside, Nish would be free. He planned on abandoning the truck in a by-lane and exiting the city, hitching a ride on one of the many vehicles going back after the immersion. If all went well, he'd be in Sri Lanka the next day, taking in the sun on Bentota beach.

Jur was sceptical of the plan, and every cell in its body rebelled against remaining immobile for hours on end. True, it would have a weapon at hand, but for the rifle was to be used the space inside the vehicle would be confined. Too many things could go wrong.

Biw, on the other hand, was quite amused by the method of travel. The sights and sounds would be worth the dismal journey. The device would need to be prepared before they started off. Biw would not allow it out of sight throughout the journey. It was waterproof, so at least that was one less thing to worry about. The time for revenge was near.

They set about making the final preparations. The plan was to start off at noon. Nish wanted them in the back of the truck in their final positions, before the team of teenagers showed up. The less the interaction, the better. He had set up a sort of curtain mounted on bamboo between the sitting space and the idol to avoid unnecessary scrutiny.

When they all agreed on the plans, they sat down to wait. With nothing else to do, Jur disassembled and cleaned its formidable-looking weapons once again. It also had a nasty-looking serrated knife it kept in a scabbard on the ankle. Nish thought about asking what the blade was for since the rifle was more than enough to cut an opponent in half. But looking at the overall demeanour of Jur, he kept his mouth shut.

Biw was setting up the device with care, occasionally consulting notes on the handheld. Nish was still not sure exactly what that machine could do, but it did not look quite so dangerous from where he sat. *Kandaarr*– that's what Biw had called it.

At 11.30 a.m. there was a sound in the yard next to the building, and the three of them became vigilant. Nish got up and opened the door just a crack, peering across the passageway to the ground. He saw the truck pull up and park.

The driver exited the cabin. Nish signalled to the two aliens and stepped out, carefully closing the door behind him. Inside, Jur stood up and slowly drew the knife from the sheath. A headache was affecting its ability to think clearly. One thing was obvious - they needed a blood sacrifice for the success of the mission.

***

As Nish came down the stairs and out in the open, the driver greeted him cheerfully, pointing out the gaily decorated trucks, completely covered in flowers and colourful cloth. Nish nodded approvingly and walked around, checking out the truck thoroughly. He liked the way the statue had been positioned. He wouldn't need to move it to make space. A couple of well-placed pieces of cloth would provide the concealment he desired.

The driver indicated he wanted to relieve himself and walked towards the side of the building. As he unzipped his pants, a figure raced down the stairs, jumped the short distance and pounced on him like a snake, and in a single stroke cut his neck from ear to ear. Jur held the driver till the body stopped shaking and then slowly dragged him under the stairs.

Nish had no time to react. He watched, open-mouthed, as Jur wiped the knife off on the driver's clothes and hid the body in the shadows. Jur raised his rifle and pointed it at him, motioning him to come closer. Though not a stranger to death, and even preparing for a genocide, this pointless murder seemed to have robbed Nish of his ability to think. Personal fear sometimes makes people act irrationally. He stumbled over to Jur, who hissed, "We take no chance. You drive."

What the hell is wrong with this guy? He's completely mental. His thoughts and actions melted into one, and he charged at Jur.

Taken by surprise, Jur staggered for a moment and dropped the rifle. Nish's hands pummelled ineffectually against the much larger Jur and his armour. Jur lashed out with one hand, catching Nish in the abdomen and as he bent down in pain, Jur reached for the rifle. Nish staggered back and through the pain kicked out Jur's legs. The two of them now rolled about in the dust, each trying to reach for a weapon. Biw had a tough time separating the two duellists. The sudden wail of a siren pierced the air and shocked the two opponents just enough that Biw could push them apart.

"Oh, hell! That's a 112!" Nish croaked out as he recognised the sound.

"What is that?"

"112 - EMRAR - Emergency First Response Automated Robotic System. The drivers' ComNet must've triggered the crisis mode. We must get out of here right now! There'll be others behind this one!"

Then the white and red '112' module came into view, flying low over the ground. EMRARs were humanoid robots with articulating arms mounted on flat pods, programmed to provide emergency medical aid by reaching accident sites within minutes.

The EMRAR's red revolving lights provided a stark contrast to the greenery in the yard as the robot homed in on the figure lying on the ground. It did not concern itself with the cause of the injury; only on the treatment required.

Jur struck out with the butt of the rifle. It caught the EMRAR just as the robot was settling down, sending it crashing into a wall. Even before the robot could recover from the blow, Jur brought the rifle crashing down again and again till only a twisted piece of plastic and metal remained.

"Let's go! Let's go! We don't have time!" Nish pulled at Biw, his anger evaporating, getting replaced with fear.

The three of them turned on their heels and rushed upstairs. It took them minutes to get all their gear loaded onto the truck and to drive out.

They met the group of boys near the main road, and everyone piled onto the back of the truck. The two aliens in their body armour lay still, down beside the idol, partially hidden by the roughly made curtain. Nish was in the cabin driving the truck. The four boys in the back were raucous and playing loud music - thus providing the perfect cover for the party.

Nish turned into the highway joining a long line of similar trucks making their way into the city. Thankfully additional EMRARs or the police had not turned up so far. They were safe. For now.

30

T Minus 10 Hours - NIA Station

Clarity of purpose drove the purposeful steps of Anara and her crew, out of the hotel and to the NIA regional office. The guards at the gate had been courteous, if disinterested, and had escorted them inside to the reception area.

They were disappointed to find that Tej was out of the office even at that early hour. The duty officer informed them she was off supervising the flushing out operations in the field and would not be back for quite some time.

They stepped back outside into the light drizzle.

"Now what do we do?" asked Anara.

"There's only one thing left to do. The mountain must go to the mahout," replied Ryan.

"You're one to expound Indian proverbs, Ryan. Anyway, that sounds logical. Let's see what our keepers have to say about this."

She went back to the guards and spoke rapidly for a few minutes. They seemed reluctant at first, but her persuasion skills were strong, and they finally relented. One of them made a call to Abhiram, and after a few minutes, Abhiram asked the trio to be brought over to the base camp near Panvel.

A short ride aboard a police car later, they touched down near the camp. The camp was, in fact, a mobile trailer, set up just off the Pune highway. There were a multitude of vehicles parked alongside, including those from the army and the air force. They had set up a rough perimeter, guarded by armed men in uniforms.

At this time of the day, the highway was deserted, and even the skies were clear of flying vehicles. It was a big holiday, and most people would be busy preparing for the prayers that evening. A couple of hyper-loop lines, passing nearby, made occasional soft whooshing sounds as they carried pods at high speed to various destinations.

They alighted their vehicle and walked to the camp. Their escorts showed their passes, and the group could step through. As they approached, the door of the trailer opened and Abhiram stepped out. He looked like he'd had a rough night. Still, his eyes were alert and showed a touch of hostility.

"What do you want, Captain?"

"We need to meet with the DG. I believe that we have information that can help you."

"Indeed?" He raised an eyebrow, clearly sceptical of their claims. "And how may I know, did you come across this information?"

"That's something I will discuss with Tej herself," replied Anara testily. She was tired of being treated in so cavalier a fashion, like a common criminal instead of a senior ranking officer. She drew herself to her full height of five feet six inches and hardened her voice. "Would you be kind enough to call her over? Or maybe it's time I started getting in touch with some people over at the ministry? I still have some hold over there, you know, being a celebrated astronaut and all that." She continued to hold Abhiram's gaze.

Abhiram may have been intimidated, but he refused to show it. He merely appraised them for a few seconds, then nodded and went back inside, closing the door behind him. The captain and her team waited expectantly, standing outside in a semicircle.

A few minutes later, they heard a craft coming in from the north. A bright speck in the sky grew progressively more substantial to reveal the latest generation Q210 tactical aircraft coming to land.

The doors of the craft opened, and Tej stepped out, this time clad in jungle textured fatigues. As she came closer, her clothes transformed to a beige colour to match the surroundings. Anara could not help feeling a twinge of jealousy watching the tall, powerful, determined figure walk towards them. Anara's own time in space had resulted in a much shorter and leaner frame; more suited for artificial gravity than lifting heavy weights on Earth.

The frown on the DG's face was visible from afar, and Anara braced herself for the inevitable confrontation.

"What do you want, Anara? I thought I'd told you to stay away from the investigation. Can't you see I'm busy trying to sort out this mess you've gotten us into?" The animosity in her voice was unmistakable.

"For starters, Tej, I need a bit more respect from you," Anara retorted adopting the same tone. "I'm not a common criminal to be treated this way. Second, I want you to understand clearly. I... did... not... bring... these... aliens... to... Earth! They would have shown up here eventually, with or without *Antariksh* going to Proxima." Ryan moved forward as if to interject himself between Anara and Tej, but Anara held him back with her left arm. "Now, the time for games is over. I ask you this - have you captured the aliens with all the fancy equipment and manpower you've got here?"

Abhiram shifted uncomfortably in his place and looked at Tej, expecting her to blow up. Instead, she smiled.

"I admire your guts, Captain. You're this close to getting arrested, despite that, you came to meet me? I'm surprised. I'd expected you to take your ship and your crew and run away." She was almost sneering.

"Well then, you're lucky, that I didn't take the simple way out, aren't you?"

The two women stood face to face in the middle of the clearing surrounded by servicemen. Neither willing to back down. The silence stretched interminable, till Ryan interrupted it with a small cough. Anara looked sideways at him and then back at Tej. She forced her body to relax. *One day, I will punch you on that pretty little nose of yours, Tej. But maybe not today.*

"We've some information that will be of use to you. I think we've identified the person who is helping the aliens and as much as it hurts me to say this, you were right." Anara took a deep breath. "It might be a member of my crew."

To Tej's credit, she did not waste time in gloating. Instead, she gestured for them to follow her inside the mobile trailer.

Once inside, she waved them to various seats around the cramped control room. Anara chose an uncomfortable chair near the door, while Ryan and Rawat preferred to remain standing.

"We have had no success in our search, and I have less than twelve hours in which to find them. Tell me what you know," ordered Tej while motioning to Abhiram to take notes.

"If that's true," said Tej as Anara finished her narrative, "then we need to lay our hands on this person, and hopefully he'll lead us straight to the aliens."

"I would assume so, but we could not locate him. His ComNet is switched off."

"ComNet tracking is for amateurs. We have something much more powerful." She nodded to Abhiram, who walked over to a technician sitting at a station and passed on instructions. "And we will talk later about this Lieutenant of yours who piggybacked onto the NIA system."

The results did not take long in coming through, and a widescreen lit up indicating locations on a map.

"ComNet for that person is inactive but these are his last known locations over the past two days. He was definitely in Mumbai when the privacy function was activated."

"Override," Tej ordered.

"Yes, ma'am. Overriding the privacy function," Abhiram instructed the tech.

"Can you guys do that - override the privacy setting, I mean?" asked Ryan, startled.

"We can override any setting, Commander. That's one privilege of being in the NIA."

"But... but isn't that illegal?"

"Seriously, Commander? Are you going to question me about legalities when thirty million lives, including yours and mine, are at stake? It would be a foolish government who would allow all controls to pass out of their hands keeping no backdoors open."

"I have overridden privacy. Waiting for a response." There was silence in the room as they watched the screen with anticipation.

"No response. The device has been physically turned off and is no longer transmitting," announced the tech.

"I was so sure this would work. Now what, Tej?" queried Anara.

"Now we use stronger measures. Abhiram, we need to activate a protocol. I'll have to brief you. Here's my reference code. Punch it in and bring up the details. Also get me the PMO."

31

T Minus 6 Hours – Highway

I *should just hand over these people to the nearest police post*, thought Nish. *It'll be so easy to end this right now. But I'm not going to do that, am I?*

He peered through the windshield at the riot of colours coursing around him: the sound of hundreds of cheerful people steeped in the moment packed into trucks and cars, blaring loud devotional music. It was enough to overwhelm all senses and precisely what Nish had been hoping for. There was no way anyone could locate them in this crowd. Despite the heavy traffic, he had made steady progress along the highway.

A posse of police and emergency response vehicles blaring sirens had passed them by some time ago. But so far no one had shown any undue interest in their vehicle.

Nish was cursing his poor judgment in aligning with the killers. Till the killing of the driver, he had looked at the entire operation abstractedly, more focused on the money than the expected loss of lives. But now he wondered if he would be able to keep his end of the bargain, knowing how utterly ruthless they were.

Were the diamonds and the promise of a kingdom enough to wipe the taint of a traitor and a genocide? Fear and greed once again fought for control in his mind. *Maybe there was a way out. Perhaps he could keep the diamonds and escape, not here, not now, but eventually. Yes, the crowds at the beach would be perfect. He could drop the aliens off, while leaving an anonymous tip for the authorities hoping they would find and defuse the device and disappear into the crowds. He had already left one clue; a couple more would seal their fate.* Having determined his course of action, he now concentrated on driving through the loud but orderly traffic, carefully avoiding the people dancing in the streets.

Jur was furious at Biw for not having finished off Nish. That is what the Chairman had wanted. Nish had caught Jur by surprise, making it drop the knife and the rifle. Half a second more and it would have cut him open end to end. Anyway, it should soon get another chance to fulfil the Chairman's orders.

Biw was silently cursing Jur. If Jur had killed Nish, they would have stood no chance of reaching the target. Biw was listening to the action that was going on all around them. *Sounds of this world before its complete annihilation.* The device was ready, and so were the two of them. The breathing apparatus had been triple checked, and the water would be a welcome break from the dry room they had been confined to for the last few days.

Another thought struck at that moment and Biw's eyes turned cold. Anger welled up again and madness gripped the mind. *Revenge. I still need my revenge. I am not done yet. Someone has to pay.*

***

The police sub-inspector walked around the body while a woman wailed in the background, held back by the police barrier. He saw the medical examiner hunched over the body. It would take some time to get more details from the ME, and the SI lifted the crime scene tape and walked back to his vehicle.

"Is that the wife, Kamble?" he asked the constable who had responded first to the accidental death report.

"*Ho, sahib,*" confirmed the constable. "Should I call her over?" For him, this case provided a well-deserved pause from the monotonous *bandobast* or security duty for the immersion.

"In a minute. Were you first on the scene? What've you done so far?"

"I received the 'injured person call' from the control room, sir. The last known location had been automatically transmitted to me. There was some delay in locating the next of kin. But Control finally contacted the wife. In the meantime, I came over and found this. It looks like he's been killed recently. His blood had just started to congeal."

"Identity?"

"A freelance driver, sir. In fact, he was supposed to be out for a run in his truck. Told his wife he'd be back only tomorrow. When the emergency signal came in, she was at the local temple. She says she missed the alert in all the chaos."

"A driver, huh? He came here in a vehicle? Where is it?"

"It's missing, sir. I have placed a lookout notice for it, but the tracker seems to be turned off. Looks like a case of simple vehicle theft, though what anyone would want with a ten-year-old truck is beyond me."

"Anything else?"

"Yes, there is actually. I found an empty transit cab, a hundred meters away, hidden in the bushes. It looks like the thieves had arrived in it, carried out the murder and left in the truck."

"Smart thieves, don't you think - exchanging a new flying taxi for a beat-up truck?" said the SI sarcastically.

"I… I didn't think of that."

The SI dismissed him and looked up at the building. *Something was not right. The place was abandoned. Derelict. Why would a truck driver come to this site at all?* He climbed up the stairs - noticing the dust had been disturbed in many places, leading up to the door of one of the rooms. As he reached the room, he dismissed the automated crime scene robots. He needed space to make his assessment. The door to the room was latched from the outside. He opened the latch and pushed the door open. The room was small and empty, but it looked like someone had been there very recently. As he examined the place, a small shining object in the corner caught his attention. It was a diamond and below it was a ComNet interface patch covered in what looked suspiciously like dried blood.

What is going on here? A diamond? Did someone drop it in this abandoned building? Why? And what about the ripped-off ComNet patch? One object was shady; two of them together were criminally suspicious. The room offered no other apparent clues, and he walked back down, allowing the crime scene robots to continue their analysis.

As he walked down the stairs, the driver's widow broke

the cordon and fell at his feet, crying bitterly. He lifted her up and led her to the ambulance nearby. As a medic handed her some water, the SI waited for her to calm down.

"Why would anyone do this, *sahib*? He never hurt anyone. What will I do now?" The wailing started afresh. The SI called over his lady constable to help comfort the wife. He needed some answers.

"Did he tell you where he was going?"

"Nothing, *sahib*. Yesterday he came home and said he had a job to carry an idol into the city for immersion. He left this morning saying he would be back late at night. I begged him not to go today, but he did not listen. The money was too good to turn down, and now he is never coming back."

A missing truck decorated for the immersion, plus a discarded ComNet suggested that someone did not want their location to be known. If he were correct, he had possibly stumbled on the hiding place of the three terrorists the alert had mentioned a couple of days back. He called this in. He needed backup and lots of it.

His Station House Officer bounced the information upwards to the area Deputy Commissioner of Police. In a matter of minutes, clearance was obtained, and a general alert was sent out to all units to keep a lookout for the truck.

A copy of the message was transmitted to the NIA which reached Abhiram instantly.

***

"Message from Mumbai Police, ma'am. They say they might've located the hideout of the suspects we'd warned them about. The place is not too far from here, near Panvel city."

"What are the source and the evidence?"

"A police sub-inspector has reported from the crime scene. He has described a stolen truck with tracking disabled and a murdered driver. They have found a… a diamond, and a discarded ComNet interface," replied Abhiram reading from the alert on the screen.

"Diamond?"

"Yes ma'am. They've also found a travel pod and are trying to trace its owner. An EMRAR sent to the spot in response to the drivers' injury was damaged as well. The local police have identified no motives or suspects, but they believe there is a link with the people we are looking for."

Tej paced around, her brows furrowed. "On the face of it there is no connection, but the local cop has acted smartly in sharing this. Get a technical team to the location right away. Tell them to first check for radiation."

"I'll also inform the police to patch the investigation updates directly to us," said Abhiram.

"Do that. We may not have much time left. This could be the break we were looking for. It can also mean that the aliens are on the move. Get in touch with the ATS. Get them to assign an armed team to us and ask the local police to get the Quick Response Teams in place. Where's my link to the PMO?" said Tej.

32

T Minus 4 Hours - The Prana Protocol

"What exactly is this *Prana* Protocol, Tej?" asked Anara.

"Nothing that you need to worry about, Captain," replied Tej offhandedly, as she manipulated the system in front of her. "It's just another government procedure."

"And what does it entail, exactly?" Anara persisted. "How will it help us in this situation?"

"Not now, Captain, I need to set this up." Her screen came alive with a logo of the PMO. Shortly she was rewarded with the image of the PM along with the CMG.

"What is it, Tej? Have you found them?" the PM asked without a preamble.

"Not yet, sir. But I have a very promising lead." She explained the circumstances in short.

"What's your plan now?"

Tej took a deep breath to steady herself. What she was

proposing was theoretically possible but had never been tried in a live situation - ever. The protocol was so secret only three people knew about it, and all three of them were connected at that moment.

"Sir, the only way I can locate them now is if I activate *Prana*."

"*Prana?*" the PM repeated, racking his memory. His face went white. *I thought that was behind me. If word of this got out, they'll throw me out of office the very next day. Who do I choose - the devil or the deep sea?* "Are you absolutely certain this is the only way?"

"I'm quite sure, sir. Once I get a fix on their location, it would be a simple matter to apprehend them before they can do any damage."

"Hold on for a moment." The screen went blank.

"What is this protocol, Tej? What could cause the PM of India to look even more worried than now?"

Tej turned around with a sigh. Fine, if Anara would not let it rest, then she would have to tell her. Either way, they would all know eventually once the protocol was activated.

"Many years ago, during the time of the terror strikes, our biggest challenge was the home-grown variety of militants. We tried everything to bust the cells, but they always seemed to be a step ahead of us. Every location we raided would be empty. We would intercept messages and track their devices, but the bad guys would go incognito before we reached anywhere near them. The privacy functions gave them the upper hand. So, we started plugging the leaks in our systems and enabled privacy override."

"The same thing you did some time back?"

"Yes. The same thing. But it wasn't enough. They learned

to deactivate the ComNet or simply go off-line after a message had been sent. Our only means of tracking them became useless. Are you following me?"

The trio surrounding her nodded, so she continued.

"Well, it was during that time that the home minister came up with a plan for a top-secret project to embed deep tracking into every communication system carried by every citizen of the country, from their birth onwards."

"Ten years ago? But that would mean our current-"

"-Prime Minister was the one who ordered the project. Yes. So now you see the reason for his anxiety. If this ever comes out, he'll be sunk - lock, stock, and no barrel."

"You already overrode some privacy controls and now this, DG? Despite all the secrecy laws protecting the citizens of the country, plus the privacy settings available on every interconnected electronic system, the government can still spy on us in multiple ways?"

Tej nodded, waiting for the screen to come alive with good news, not bothering to reply to the obvious.

"And how does it work? Does it override the privacy settings or what?"

"No. Like I'd said, that wouldn't work if the devices were powered down. Instead, they came up with a plan that made it mandatory for every communication system to be embedded with a small dormant chip. This chip is not connected to any power source, nor does it transmit any signals. It's completely passive. It is invisible unless someone takes apart the system at molecular level."

"If it's dormant, it wouldn't work once the system was powered down, would it?"

"Not necessarily. You see, these chips are electromagnetic responders. We embedded reading antennas in all the communication towers and satellites. Now these reading antennae are also completely powered down and emit no signals. They work independent of the standard ComNet. But once energised, like we are going to do now, they will send out electromagnetic waves of a specific excitation frequency. The passive chips in the ComNets will absorb this electromagnetic energy and in turn, the chips will get sufficient power to transmit their positions."

"Allowing you to track every single person whether they are connected to the network or powered down." Anara struggled to come to terms with this invasion of privacy which went against every grain of decency and ethics. *Would anyone be crazy enough to defy the laws of the land on this scale?*

"Millions of people simultaneously- if required, though in a localised area only," said Tej casually shrugging her shoulders, ignoring the shocked expression on Anara's face. "Unfortunately, we've never tested the system in real time. One can't help but admire the simplicity of the system. No one needs to know anything until we activate the system. And it can track all living human beings. Hence the code name '*Prana*' - life."

"I… I don't know what to say, Tej. I never expected my government to be behind a conspiracy of this magnitude. How do you people even go to sleep at night?"

"It's all right for you to pontificate morality, Anara. You're not responsible for the lives of millions of citizens. Step into my shoes and then maybe you'll understand. It's all for the greater good. Besides, it's nothing new. Governments across the world are obsessed with keeping tabs on our enemies.

Ours is just one of them. Privacy, my dear captain, has been and will always be a myth. Remember that."

"Is there any way the person being tracked would know that the device has been activated?" asked Ryan.

Tej smiled. "The one fatal flaw in the system, Commander. Once energised, the chip absorbs a sizable amount of energy and gets hot. It essentially burns out the person's ComNet system. It wouldn't take a rocket scientist to figure out the reason for the burning out of so many ComNets at the same time. The secret would come out even if the protocol is used even once. It would also alert the enemy. That's the reason it has never been used or tested on a large scale. Of course, it only affects personal ComNets, not the police, army and a few others."

The screen buzzed behind her. "It does give us a small window of opportunity. Burn them and take them out. Now if you'll excuse me," said Tej as she turned her back on them.

"Yes, Mr. Prime Minister?" she said to the figure on the screen.

There was some incomprehensible reply from the screen.

"Right, sir. Thank you. We'll get them now. Tej out."

She turned around, and her eyes found Abhiram's. "*Prana* is a go, Abhiram. The operational sequence is being shared with you right now. Get your team to initialise the signals. In the meantime, get the ATS to backtrack the places Nish had visited before he deactivated his signal. We need more confirmation that he is the double agent. I don't want to run down this path and then realise we've been chasing the wrong person."

With a rational purpose ahead of her, Tej seemed intensely focused. "Captain, it'll take some time to get the towers and satellites activated before we can start collecting the data. Come wait with me and let's see if you were right?"

***

In the CMG room in Delhi, the PM turned towards his advisors. "There is no turning back now. It's done." He walked back wearily to his seat knowing well that the opposition would allow him to continue in office once they knew the truth. He sighed. *I am getting too old for this stuff, anyway. Maybe it was time I retired. Yes, once this was over. Let someone else deal with the aftermath.*

"Sir?" the home minister spoke up, causing the PM to snap out of his reverie. He raised an eyebrow.

"Now that we know the aliens are in Mumbai and possibly headed into the city, I think it is time to order the evacuation." Sullen faces nodded gravely around the room. They had to cut losses should Tej fail.

"I had given the NIA forty-eight hours to find the aliens before I ordered evacuation. There is still some time to go."

"If the aliens are already inside the city, I'm afraid we don't have a few hours, sir. We need to advance the schedule. We should at least move the troops to their final positions and get the local government and high-risk areas secured."

The PM signed again, "Which are the areas at maximum risk?"

"We had already decided that during our planning, sir."

"Tell me again. Which are the high-risk areas?"

"Maximum population density is from Dadar southwards. Also, the south Mumbai beaches will be crowded with Ganpati processions."

"Ok. But let's start only with the Mantralaya and Shivaji Nagar before we cause widespread panic. Get everyone out from the underwater city through the sea routes. You have my go ahead. I'll inform the chief minister."

The order for evacuation was on its way to the military commander in charge of Operation *Moksh*. Within minutes, vessels under the naval command started heading towards the embarkation points of the underwater city.

***

They had arrived in twos and threes, meeting up in the various cafes that dotted the roads near the Gateway of India. Staying in touch through text messages, the team leaders had been busy keeping their respective flocks together. Keith saw the growing numbers with satisfaction. *Another couple of hours and they will be ready to go.*

He was standing outside the cafe, looking at the gaily dressed crowds of devotees all moving towards the seashore a few miles away. He had never really understood the way the Indians insisted on making all their festivals noisy and colourful. Every ceremony was like a never-ending party. Yet, somehow, the piety of the faithful still shone through.

He flicked his wrist to turn on the time display. Just a few more hours. His lieutenants would meet him once their people had assembled. They would start moving in a direction opposite to the immersion crowds - down Colaba market, exiting the shopping row and towards the hospital. He was hoping to have at least a thousand people assembled. That would be more than enough to storm the hospital and get the aliens. His careful preparations so far had ensured that the police had no inkling of the force that was about to overwhelm them. The best part was that everyone was busy with the processions and the immersions. Nobody would pay attention to another thousand people till it was too late.

33

T Minus 4 Hours - Marine Drive

The codes for activating *Prana* were sent over from the PMO on a secure channel to the NIA control centre. From that point, it took several minutes to enable the control towers to transmit the energising signal. Towers across the city and multiple satellites in the sky came alive with a new type of EM-pulse.

When the radio waves from the readers reached the ComNet devices embedded in the citizens, they activated the hidden chips. These started emitting a magnetic field. This secondary signal reached back to the towers and satellites, thus signalling the presence of specific individuals and pinpointing their location. The accuracy of the position was limited because of the technology used, but a fix of every individual was available with an accuracy of one hundred meters. In almost all the cases, the chips burnt out as well causing annoyance if not pain to many individuals.

Millions of signals started flowing into the control centre

and were swiftly catalogued by the computer with the name and identity of every citizen. Nish's details had already been fed into the computer, but it did not get any matches. He had not been located. The NIA's gambit with *Prana* had failed.

***

A call went out to Tej, and the tech apprised her of the findings. The group huddled around her. Their last hope was heading for failure. Then Ryan finally homed in on what had been troubling him.

"Hold on, guys. We are forgetting something. The police had found a ComNet patch at that place in Panvel, right? Have they determined who it belongs to?"

"No, not yet, Commander. It is a little tricky analysing a patch once it has been removed."

"But if it belongs to Nish, as we suspect, then even if we track it with *Prana*, it'll not help us track his real-time movements, right?"

"That's correct, although I have data on his movements over the last few hours. He was definitely in Mumbai, and a team from the ATS is tracing his steps. We should get an update soon," replied Abhiram, not sure where Ryan was leading them.

"That's good. But coming back to the original ComNet. It would have lost power once it's removed and it wouldn't show up at all. But he had a secondary chip - just like all of us who had been part of the mission with ISC. That would have a different identity module. We need to look for that chip."

"Of course." Tej cursed herself silently for having missed this crucial point. "We will need the ID number. Can you get it?"

"Narada will draw that out. Give me a minute." Anara was

already on the system talking to Narada. She relayed the information to the control centre as fast as Narada called it out.

"I've got him!" They all heard the exultant voice of the tech in the control centre. "He is somewhere near Babulnath Road, Girgaum, South Mumbai."

"You know what this means, don't you, Abhiram?"

"Yes, ma'am. It means that Nish is leading us to the aliens. But since he removed the patch instead of just turning off the privacy function, it also means that he does not want to be captured himself. Mr. Nish is playing a dangerous double game."

***

The crowds grew progressively more abundant as the truck crossed the two refurbished sea links connecting the north of Mumbai to the south. Nish had managed to get them to Chowpatty without being detected.

He slowly eased the truck into the designated parking lot near the immersion point on the beach. Massive crowd-control towers floated in the air while multiple human volunteers and official robots directed the crowds down predetermined paths to the immersion points. The roads and sidewalks had been cleared and temporary cordons set up. Climate control had been turned off in the area and nature was being allowed to take its course. What was immersion without rain? And this rain suited his plans perfectly.

The backdrop of the skyscrapers, rising hundreds of meters in the sky, behind them provided a perfect setting for the loud cries of *'Ganpati Bappa Morya'* - Glory to Lord Ganpati - intermingled with the sounds of cymbals and drums. The drums were noteworthy - every group seemed to have their own drummer, but the overall effect was one of harmony instead of a cacophony.

Nish wandered off to arrange an anti-gravity sled. Once he came back, they carefully lifted down the idol and the much more burdensome demons/aliens and arranged them nicely. It was tough for the aliens to remain still and not be discovered but with much pushing, pulling and grunting Nish and the youth succeeded.

Their little procession, one among many, moved off slowly, meandering down the road. Many in the crowd marvelled at the lifelike display - a god defeating demon-like aliens.

Nish soon stopped worrying about getting rid of his boy gang. Like most youngsters caught up in the exuberance of the moment, they had melted away into the crowds, dancing away to the rhythmic beating of the drums. This time he would not have to prevent Jur from murdering another four innocent people. That was getting tiresome and a little scary - Jur had no morals or compulsions about taking any lives.

All alone now, he raised the anti-gravity sled a little more and kept on moving with the crowd. In typical Mumbai fashion, forged over many, many decades, once you became part of a line you did not need to make any further efforts - the crowd took care of you. You became one in a microcosm.

A couple of hundred yards further and he was at the edge of the water. Two rigger robots helped slide the statue and accessories onto the floating platform which would take it further out into the sea. One rigger reminded him that plastic could not be cast into the sea. He acknowledged the instructions and removed the accessories, leaving only the armour on the bodies of the aliens

The rain was pelting down now, and visibility was nearly down to zero. Nish climbed onto the platform and pushed it off, guiding the two small outboard motors, till they reached twenty meters inside the sea. From there, it was a short matter to push the idol into the water where it would dissolve in a few minutes. The two TrueKifs slid off on their own and stayed underwater. Nish gave a last look around to ensure that no one was watching them; and then he too jumped into the water.

34

T Minus 3 Hours – The Search

The quadcopters, full of NIA personnel and ATS commandos, lifted off one by one and headed straight to the heart of the city. High priority flying lanes had been cleared for their travel to Chowpatty beach.

Within the lead chopper, Tej and Abhiram were on separate systems rapidly issuing multiple orders to their teams on the ground. Every available asset was being rushed to the area, but her call with the Commissioner of Police was not going well.

"I'm telling you, Commissioner, these guys are armed and extremely dangerous. I need every available person to search for them." She was senior to that man, but this was not the time to pull ranks.

"And I am telling you, madam, today is *visarjan* day. Millions of people have congregated in the area you are mentioning. I've already handed over the ATS and QRTs to you. I don't have anyone left to spar"

"What about your drones and the security robots?"

"All the drones are engaged in crowd monitoring and control. Not to forget, I am supposed to be working on the evacuation as well. Look here, I know what you're trying to do, and you have my complete support. I'm not trying to stonewall you, but my cupboard is empty."

"Just give me access to the data from your drones. I'll search on my own."

"That won't work. You'd be looking for facial recognition or close-ups while we need high-level views to manage bottlenecks and ensure the crowds keep moving. Do you even understand the logistical nightmare I'm dealing with here?"

"I don't care about your damned traffic, Commissioner!" Tej finally lost her cool. "All of this will be in vain if those three get away from me now. I'm telling you for the last time - if they escape, it'll be on your head alone. I can get the Chief Minister online to give direct instructions if you want."

There was silence on the line, and she could visualise the uniformed officer sitting in his own control centre fighting his anger. But she was right, and he would know that.

"I'll see what I can do," he finally replied stiffly and signed off.

"We have access," announced Abhiram a couple of minutes later. "The commissioner has also released additional police units to our command."

"Remind me to thank him later. He has taken a gamble for us. For now, get every drone on face scanning mode. Recall others in the general area to Marine Drive. Find them."

***

With time to go before his team made its move, Keith lounged in the shadow of a pillar in front of the cafe. His vigil over the last few hours had revealed no threats to his plan. He was itching to go ahead now.

A few low-flying drones were keeping a close eye on the festivities and probably transmitting to the central control room. Armed police officers, accompanied by robot crowd controllers, stood around on the sidewalk. They seemed bored. The crowd was peaceful, if a little boisterous, and the police had little to do.

There was a commotion, and to Keith's surprise, he saw the drones abruptly rise and disappear to the north. The police officers on the sidewalk became alert, listening to orders coming in through their earpieces. Their sub-inspector seemed to acknowledge some commands, for he turned around and barked at her squad. A ground vehicle pulled up next to them, and they climbed aboard. The vehicle turned north, blaring sirens and scattering people in the path. It shortly disappeared around the corner. Just two officers were left behind.

Across the area, he could hear more sirens. Many people seemed to look around trying to see where this sudden commotion was coming from. But as the sirens faded in the distance, the crowd went back to its business. The uproar was forgotten.

Incredible. Even the gods are with me today. He had just gained a few extra minutes. Keith called up his team leaders and told them to move.

Slowly, trying not to draw attention, his crowd started off down the road - determined and convinced of the sanctity of their task.

***

"The drones have not returned any positive IDs, ma'am."

"What about the location tracking? Are they still moving?" Tej asked as she looked at her own screen following the path of the blip.

"We're a little hampered. The accuracy is not great. I had them moving towards the sea some time back. Let me try another active ping," replied the tech. The signal was sent, but there was no response. He tried again. No result. "I'm sorry ma'am, I've lost them."

"What do you mean - lost them?" Tej thundered.

The technician quailed.

"There is no response," he stammered out. "The signal is gone."

"Ping again."

"Yes, ma'am." The technician tried again. "Still no response. The chip will most probably have burnt out or maybe they have gone underwater?" he suggested.

"There is a call from the control room. They have successfully located the radiation signals. Madhavan is sending the data now." Abhiram expanded the screen and projected it. "Radiation traces at three positions. Here, here and here," he said, pointing to the map.

"The first one was at Panvel, right where they found the body. The second - Chowpatty and the third in the Arabian Sea. Extrapolate with the *Prana* locations, Abhiram."

New location symbols were inter-laid on the radiation markers, and the two women nodded to each other. They were close to the aliens but where exactly were the mercenaries now?

35

T Minus 2 Hours – The Underwater City

I *Miscalculated. I should have known that I could not leave them at the pier. I will have to wait for the next opportunity at the underwater city.*

As Nish entered the water, his action drew the attention of an EMRAR, which interpreted this behaviour as an accident. It flew over their position and dropped a signal buoy in the water. Nish saw this and realised that rescue teams would reach there in minutes. He pulled out his breathing appliance and put it in his mouth. It closed over his nose, and the breathing tube would allow him to swim unhindered for a few hundred meters. He slipped off his shoes and dunked his head into the water, shivering now from the continuous exposure to rain and cold sea water. *This will be over in a few minutes. I need to hang on for a bit more.*

The TrueKifs swam ahead comfortably, coming up for air only at very long intervals. Jur took point, powerful strokes from its six limbs covered the distance rapidly.

***

Behind them automated SAR, search and rescue, teams converged near the platform and started a systematic grid-based search. Radar and sonar continuously pinged the sea to locate their bodies while a coast guard boat stood a hundred meters off to assist if called for. The surface of the sea rolled incessantly, and the rain hampered the effectiveness of the robots.

***

The three of them kept swimming carefully, conserving energy, until they reached the breakwater, about fifty yards from the edge of the city. As they entered the sheltered cove beyond the breakwater, they saw the lights of the city for the first time, glowing eerily in the darkness of the water surrounding it.

***

The city had been built after dredging out parts of the continental shelf and covered an area of roughly five square kilometres with a maximum depth of thirty meters. It would remain submerged during high tide, while at low tide, the top of the dome could be seen rising above the water. The vast dome was made of transparent metal, supported by struts made of carbon nanotubes. It could withstand super cyclonic storms or category 7 hurricanes, becoming flexible during a storm or made to remain rigid when the sea was calm. While flexible, it would move with the waves, providing an ethereal effect when viewed from inside. The city was self-sufficient - from fresh air pumped in by massive ventilators to power from tidal generators and clean water from reclamation systems.

***

The three of them reached the edge of the city and rested against the bottom of the struts supporting the dome under the sea. All that remained now was to find an entry inside. Nish gestured to the other two, and they slowly circled the dome, looking for an ingress point. It was easy enough to find one, clearly marked as the emergency exit, with an airlock, most likely connected to an alarm system. The door could not be opened from outside except with brute force.

Jur moved ahead and unslung the rifle from its back. The other two stepped aside to give a wide berth as it pointed the gun at the edge of the door and pressed the trigger. A thin red beam of a high-powered laser hit the door and cut clean through it. The door slowly swung open; the lock sheared clean from the frame. A rotating red warning light, indicating a breach, came on. Biw nodded to Jur and moved ahead to enter the airlock and Nish made to follow. He felt a hand on his shoulder and turned his head slowly in exasperation - probably Jur wanting to enter the city before him.

The murky water masked the look of surprise in his eyes when Jur held both of Nish's hands in its own and used a third to yank out the breathing apparatus. Nish struggled frantically against the brawny arms holding him, while his legs banged ineffectually against the seabed raising clouds of sand. Jur did not slacken the grip till a cloud of bubbles burst forth from Nish's mouth, and his body went limp.

Jur continued the hold for another minute while retrieving the pouch with the diamonds. Nish's body went completely limp, and Jur slowly released it, allowing it to float away free. Death for Nish had come abruptly, and no one would ever know what he had done or why.

***

Jur entered the airlock behind Biw and slammed the door shut then sealed it with a burst from the rifle. It nodded to Biw, who pressed the release button allowing the water to be pumped out. As compressed air flooded the compartment, Biw trembled involuntarily. Jur had killed two people in one day without a hint of remorse, and now the bloodlust in the eyes was unmistakable. *Ignore these thoughts. I need revenge as much as Jur does and if they lose here a few lives, so be it.*

The two of them entered an empty maintenance corridor and found another door marked 'Exit' right in front of them. The letters glowed yellow on green while the passage itself was lit dimly with the diffused glow from ceiling lights set across the length. It seemed to curve around the entire city.

The second door brought them out into the principal thoroughfare, which circled the city. Across the street, they could see the lights of the city itself stretching out as far as the eyes could see. The vaulted ceiling rising many meters above the ground provided a sinister backdrop to what they were about to perpetrate. They nearly smiled at the setting for the calamity that would ensue soon.

There was, however, something that bothered Biw. It was too quiet. There were no people, no vehicles, and absolutely no sound. The city was deserted.

They stumbled across the road confused.

"Where is everybody, Biw? Nish said there would be thousands of people here." Jur felt betrayed. They had not travelled billions of miles for this.

"I don't know! I don't know!" Biw screamed back, equally frustrated as he kicked a dustbin standing by the side of the road. The glass windows of the row of shops lining the side of the road were all dark. The doors were locked and shuttered. "Do you think they have located us and evacuated the place?"

For once it was right on the mark - the city had been the first place to be evacuated. It had taken just two hours to get everyone out and enforce a complete lockdown. Had they been topside a little earlier, they would have seen the unending stream of ships fleeing the city as the navy took control. Most people had been out in the city for the *visarjan*, and it had been easier to evacuate the diminished population.

"What the hell do we do now?"

***

"Ma'am, I was scanning the alerts from the beach. There's a report of a man who drowned in the sea a short while ago. It seems he left his vehicle behind. The police are there now, and they seem to have found some leads."

"Do you have visuals?"

"Coming right up," said the tech as the screen filled with visuals from the first responder EMRAR. A face was clearly visible for a moment before it vanished below the waves.

"That's Nish," confirmed Rawat. "Can we tap into visuals from security cams in the area a few minutes before this happened?"

The tech nodded and manipulated the controls. The visuals changed and flowed back in time as they followed the agent's progress in reverse.

"Stop right there! Those shapes - zoom in," ordered Tej. The view resolved into a clear shot of the idol and the two statues under it. "Well, it's clear now how they entered

Mumbai. No wonder they escaped detection. Couldn't have managed it without inside help. You've trained your people well, Major," she said drily.

***

"I don't know what we should do now. Maybe if you had not killed Nish, we would have had an alternate plan!" Biw faced off with Jur.

"Don't take that tone with me," warned Jur. "He's better off dead. They will find his body and assume we all drowned in the sea. We need to finish our mission. I will not be denied again."

"Oh, yeah? You think the Earth people are so stupid to believe that we all drowned together?" The reply dripped with sarcasm. "You are a bloody brute, and you have completely messed up our mission. First HuZryss and now this. You are pathetic!"

"I am warning you, Biw! You're going too far. Shut up or…"

"Or what, Jur? Will you kill me too just like you killed the other two? Who will set up your bomb then, huh? You know nothing about that. I can't believe the Chairman chose you for this mission." Biw was deliberately pushing Jur over the edge. A little bit more and Jur would turn over to the new option. "You think I'm afraid of you? Come on, and let's find out who deserves the Chairman's trust more!"

***

There's something else, ma'am. The SAR teams have located a body near the underwater city. It's the same person we were looking for, Mr. Nish."

"Nish? Dead?" Tej was incredulous. "How did that happen?"

"Looks like he drowned but they need time to be sure."

"What about his accomplices?"

"There are no reports on the aliens accompanying him or any other bodies. Sorry."

"Do you think they've entered the underwater city?" asked Abhiram.

"It might've been their primary target. How many people inside, Abhiram? Can we get them all out?"

"Let me check." He called up the latest stats on the city. "Er…. That may not be necessary. We received a message some time back. I seemed to have missed it. They evacuated the city an hour ago. It's empty, ma'am. There's no one there. Unfortunately, no one seems to have thought of preventing unauthorised access."

"Oh. A step ahead and a step behind. That's good. A few thousand souls less to worry about. That gives us some breathing space. How long before we reach Marine Drive?"

"Three minutes," replied her pilot.

"Change flight path. Let's get to the underwater city directly. Divert half the squad to the beach. Tell them to search the beach and the water with the 'bots'. The rest will come with us. Call ACP Shinde and ask him to meet us with additional commandos at the city gates."

"Yes, ma'am." Abhiram rapidly fired off the instructions and relayed the request. By this time, they had reached their destination, and their copter lost altitude to land in front of the causeway leading to the underwater city. A second chopper with a section of commandos landed right beside them. The third copter with half their commando squad had peeled off earlier and headed for Chowpatty beach.

The Force One commandos exited the craft swiftly and ran ahead. Tej and her team were right behind them. Another craft landed softly, and ACP Shinde joined them with a few more troops.

The gates of the city were blocked by two armoured cars, along with a couple of platoons of the army and an equal number of local police. Tej had a rapid exchange with the DCP in charge at the entrance of the underwater city and they opened the gates to allow them inside.

***

"Years and years of preparation–wasted. You are sure the warning did not reach him?" '5' screamed at his intelligence team.

"No sir, it did not. By the time we got the details from the NIA and tried, the communication network had collapsed. We do not know what happened, but it is unlikely he has received our message."

"Very well, he may have been condemned by his fate, but we still have our task to complete. We must move up the schedule for the launch of our ship. If the device is still undamaged, then we can still secure it. We cannot fail again."

36

T Minus 2 Hours –
The Escape

The mild ache had transformed into a pounding in Jur's head. Strength seemed to leaving its body slowly. "Why don't we just go back to the beach? We can explode the bomb there." There were enough people on the beach.

"That's not good enough; the place will be swarming with men looking for us. We can't go back. I won't get enough time to set it up."

"You can set off the device underwater."

"No, I can't. It will not be effective. The water will dampen the explosion. Now keep quiet and let me think."

"Don't order me around. I am not your slave!"

"No, you are not. You are just a fool." Biw couldn't help goading it further. This stupid oaf had spoiled plans that had been carefully laid out.

Jur snapped again. With a roar of rage, it sprang forward, and in a trice, its fingers were closing on Biw's neck. Biw tried to resist the grip, but Jur was too strong. Everything went black. One hand came down and fingered the weapon on the waist. With nothing left to lose, the gun came out, and fired a single shot. It entered Jur's leg just above the knee. It howled in pain and released the pressure on Biw's neck. Biw staggered back, taking deep gasps of air, still holding the gun.

"Never do that again; otherwise I swear I will kill you," Biw gasped out. "And take away your hands from that rifle."

Jur, who had just started reaching for its weapon, stopped moving. The pain in its leg threatened to overcome its anger. There was no mistaking the malevolent look in its eyes.

"You will get us killed, Jur. Earth security will be here soon. We need to leave now. There is nothing more we can do here." Time to bring out the final bait. Aloud he said, "We have to find Joe and Lucy. Nish said they were at a hospital somewhere nearby. He gave me the coordinates."

Jur just glared back at him. "You have disregarded every order given by the Chairman. The hospital is not our primary objective."

"It is now, Jur and we need to leave immediately. Someone will have heard the shot. They will come to investigate. We'll figure out the route on the way. It is going to be a long swim."

***

They entered the deep cavern on foot. The ATS team followed Tej and turned left on the causeway. The local police team from the barricade turned right. Anara ran to keep up with her group led by Tej. It was deathly quiet inside and they heard the shot clearly.

"That was a gunshot. Someone's here. Go! Go! Go!"

The soldiers broke their ranks into multiple two-member teams, running into the by-lanes while others continued down the main road at a fast jog. Anara and Ryan were left far behind, but Rawat could keep up with the troopers. As he ran ahead, a handgun appeared in his right hand.

Panting for breath, Anara finally caught up with them a kilometre ahead. She found Rawat and ACP Shinde standing together examining the ground. Rawat held an alien helmet in his hand and showed it to Anara.

"They were definitely here," said Rawat. "We must've missed them by minutes. The soldiers have gone around looking for them. I don't know what happened here or who was shooting at who, but we found some blood stains here."

Signals of 'all clear' came through their headpieces as the troops cleared the buildings. This did not take too much time as most of them were locked. Finally, all the teams checked in with the ACP with negative sightings. The aliens were gone.

"We've lost them again. It was so close this time. The soldiers are still checking the whole city, but that'll take time," said Tej as she came back. "They couldn't have gotten away too far." She sipped water from a bottle borrowed from a serviceman while looking around to find Abhiram.

The ACP finished his conversation and joined her. "They are no longer here. I think they've slipped off into the sea through one of the emergency escapes. I've called the navy and coast guard for help. They have some ships around. Let's get back to the quadcopter. I need to start the search and coordinate with the navy."

***

"What do you think happened here?" asked Anara.

Tej was thinking precisely along these lines as she walked. They had observed two aliens at the beach in the surveillance videos. Nish had accompanied them. *But Nish was dead. Was that an accident or had he been murdered?*

"I think Nish's utility for the aliens was over and they got rid of him. They did not know that Shivaji Nagar had been evacuated. They were most probably surprised and spooked at the same time or maybe they had a falling out. The problem is that with Nish's death we've now lost our only method of tracking them. They could be anywhere in the city by now. The good news is that Operation *Moksh* is being extended. They'll be clearing the city block by block. but we need to give them more time. If we can pin the location of the aliens or just keep them moving, that will keep them from exploding the bomb or whatever they have planned to do."

But this was easier said than done. They needed another break. It was now a race against time.

***

Keith had almost six hundred people so far, walking down the road nonchalantly. They looked just like groups of tourists enjoying the holy day, trying not to attract much attention. It annoyed him that the crowd was smaller than he had expected. There seemed to be some trouble in the city and roads were being blocked, trapping the rest of his team just a couple of miles away. It doesn't matter; he had enough for his plan to work.

The peaceful nature of the crowd would change once they reached the hospital gates. His core team was dispersed in the crowd and would swing into action the moment he gave the signal. It was kind of the police to have cooperated with him. They were moving ahead with practically no surveillance.

Keith increased his pace as he sought to reach the front of the assembly. He had to be inside the moment his team broke through. Finding the exact room would not be difficult since he knew the rough location by heart. Aisha had told him that the security was light. The guards would be prepared for a limited engagement but certainly not for a mob attack. Anyway, she had promised to meet him in the corridor outside and guide him if required. He had never been inside the hospital but knew how easy it would be to get lost inside a large unknown facility. He needed the nurse's help.

A few more minutes and they would be near their objective. He did not anticipate getting stopped anymore since the military restrictions around the area had been lifted many years back. But precautions were necessary for success.

He bent his head against the strong wind and heavy rain and plodded onward.

***

In another part of the city, with definite data in hand, the ATS was backtracking Nish's movements. The large transfer of money from his account to another had showed up. From that point it was a simple matter to put two and two together. The nearest police station and Force One teams were alerted. They needed to take down a suspect.

***

Karam had pulled down the shutters early like the rest of the city on visarjan day. No one was going to go out shopping today, and he did not see any point in keeping up appearances. He sat in his chair behind the counter and poured himself a drink. He needed it today. The assignment with Nish had netted him a tidy profit, and he'd already checked out the betting odds for the upcoming one-day cricket matches in September.

The shuttered door of his shop blew apart causing him to

drop his drink in panic. Multiple hooded and black-clad figures clambered in through the now splintered entrance. He jumped out of his chair and fell on the floor, covering his head with his hands. He did not even get to look up as the cold barrel of a gun was placed on his temple.

"Well, well, Karam." The voice was familiar. "Remember, I had warned you that one day you'd go too far. What have you done this time to get the NIA interested in your piddly operation?"

"Inspector Kale? You? I don't know what you mean! I've not done anything!"

"Is that so? Then you won't mind me looking through your internal surveillance footage, would you?"

"Surveillance footage? I don't have any video cameras, sir. I'm a poor man."

"Shut it. I'll come to the point. We're looking for Nish. He came here two days ago. I need that video. I also need to know what you sold him - guns, drugs, explosives?" The inspector kept his hand on Karam's head and grabbed a handful of hair. "Will you talk here, or do you want to go to the NIA centre?" The threat of the NIA was enough to drain the blood from his face. *Oh shit, Nish. What've you gotten me into this time?*

Karam started talking, and he did not stop for a full ten minutes. That was enough for the inspector to find and check the surveillance tapes. He gestured to his team, and Karam was unceremoniously hauled to his feet and taken away in handcuffs.

The inspector called up Abhiram. "His story checks out. Nish was here. I'm sending the footage. It seems Karam helped him convert some money. But I think he was also telling the truth when he said he wasn't aware what Nish was up to."

"Ok, Inspector. I'm also sending you the details of the transport pod we found in Panvel. Records show it was last given for overhaul in your general area. I suggest you follow up the lead and see what you can find. Report back as soon as possible."

***

"I think we can safely say that we've got identification of the man for whatever it is worth, now that he is dead," Abhiram reported grimly to his boss.

37

T Minus 0 - INHS Asvini

Lucy was sleeping peacefully. *This has gone off better than I expected,* thought Dr. Khan. The baby was strong and healthy. He was confident that baby Anara would adapt and grow up to be an active and healthy woman.

Joe also stood to one side watching the nurse fuss over the sleeping form. *Aisha is full of nervous energy today,* Joe thought, watching her move around non-stop. *Must be something to do with the birth of a celebrity.*

"You can take a break, nurse," said Dr. Khan. "I am sure they'll be fine."

Aisha gave him a small smile. "It's all right, Doctor. I will be off duty in a couple of hours. Besides, I'm used to this." Dr. Khan nodded and went back to his ruminations.

*****

It had been a hard, long swim for Jur and Biw in the choppy waters. They had kept away from the shallows and did not get any opportunity to rest. Fortunately, the familiarity they had with water back on KifrWyss had helped them make the trip with relative ease. The heavy pack on the back had given Biw some trouble. With Jur sulking, injured and refusing to help, Biw struggled to manage the swim.

Somehow, after an hour, crossing the reef and turning left, they were in sight of the hospital. The open ground next to the seashore looked deserted. Only a low metal fence guarded it and the rocky beach would provide them easy access inside. They moved forward cautiously and came to rest at the edge of the shoreline. They observed the building silently, keeping their heads just under the water.

It was an imposing multi-story building with two wings from what they could observe. They were sure Lucy and Joe would be in one of the main sections. Conversing in a low voice, they split up. Biw would take the building on the left while Jur would search the one on the right. With any luck, they would be able to locate the two people and be ready to escape back to their mother ship. Jur pulled on the body armour while Biw watched, not bothering to don his own suit.

It was dark, and the heavy rain masked their approach to the fence. Both gripped the heavy rods and swung themselves up slowly, stepping onto the wet grass. They weren't aware that an intruder alarm went off in the hospital control room.

***

Keith's people were all in position, and it was time for action. The gates of the hospital were wide open, and he could only see one unarmed guard standing beside them. Keith raised his hand and gave the signal to the core team.

Looking entirely benign, two members of his group walked up to the gate and engaged the guard in conversation. *We're tourists, you see. We seem to have lost our way in the crowds and we need to get back to our hotel near the Gateway. Can you guide us?*

As the guard answered the queries, one man reached from behind and grabbed his arms while the second punched him straight in the face. The guard went down like a ton of bricks, and they eased him to a side. The next few events happened rapidly.

Keith ran across the road and entered the path leading to the hospital flanked by two people on each side. His target was in the wing on the left. Behind him a horde of demonstrators broke out of the shadows and shouting slogans, the mob entered the premises en masse.

***

The perimeter breach alarm and the sudden appearance of seemingly thousands of people at the main gate startled the Sub-Lieutenant on duty. His training kicked, and he pushed the master alarm that would signal personnel across the compound to go for a lock-down while simultaneously alerting the force guarding the complex. He did not know what this was all about, but it was his duty to protect everyone on campus. He then left the room in the hands of the Chief Petty Officer, telling her to ensure the door was locked behind him and rushed off to the main entrance. The mob had to be tackled first.

***

Jur and Biw had just reached the rear portico when the blaring sirens broke through the howling of the wind and rain. They needed to move fast. The first resistance they met was two armed guards at the rear entrance. But even as the guards overcame their surprise at the sight of a four-handed 'demon' and reached for their weapons, Jur opened fire with the rifle. The powerful rounds blew a hole through one guard who died instantly. The other guard turned and tried to run for cover, but a second round caught him in the back of his head, which exploded from the impact. Biw turned around at this sight and fell, retching loudly. So much blood.

"Get up, you *kychol!*" shouted Jur in contempt and pulled Biw to his feet with two free hands. "We have much more killing to do."

Somehow finding strength and wiping vomit, Biw staggered behind Jur. They pushed open doors at random, sending startled staff and civilians running for cover.

This is the enemy. They are the ones who came to KifrWyss and humiliated me. This is my time for revenge. Jur went into autopilot mode. The rifle barked again and again. Bodies fell in its path.

Biw had gotten separated from Jur and ran from door to door, not bothering with killing anyone. *Where were Lucy and Joe?*

***

The quadcopter circled the sea, trying to assist the naval armada in their search for the aliens. Visibility was abysmal, and a visual search was impossible. Even sonar and infrared were being hampered by the rough sea and the falling rain. Nevertheless, they had persisted. An incoming message from Naval Command broke through their routine.

"Copy that. I'll get back to you. Hope riot control is on the way?" said the ACP. "There is a break-in at INHS Asvini. A perimeter breach, reports of a mob storming the complex. They're dispatching forces." Anara's eyes went wide.

"Coincidence, do you think?" asked Tej, looking at the ACP.

"Not in our business, DG ma'am. That hospital is housing two 'new' humans. How and why did the mob get there? There must be some connection. What if the aliens have reached there? It has been more than an hour since we lost them in the underwater city. We need to get there now!"

"I agree. Abhiram, get the control room to focus their radiation search in the Colaba area to confirm. Pilot, get us to INHS Asvini. ACPji, do you have any other troops available?"

"No more ATS commandos, ma'am. But the NSG black cat commandos were assigned to that sector. I'll get them moving right away."

The quadcopter turned in mid-air and finding a new heading flew out at maximum thrust, its engines screaming in the night. A second quad carrying a complement of the ATS commandos followed them.

***

The mob had overwhelmed the guards at the main gate easily and had almost reached the front porch. Armed naval ratings led by the Sub-Lieutenant rushed through the entrance almost at the same time but hesitated briefly in the face of the concerted assault. Then he and his troops had formed a cordon, raised their rifles and fired warning shots over the heads of the protestors. The answer came in the form of flash-bang grenades and Molotov cocktails, but some of the crowd scattered, and the front of the building burst into flames as the doors caught fire.

With the firing inside and outside the building, complete mayhem had broken out in the complex. The staff and patients inside tried to escape the aliens by rushing out while the mob outside again tried to storm in. The Sub-Lieutenant stared at the carnage in disbelief. He heard a shout behind him and found his commander coming to his aid with another squad of sailors.

They rushed past him and engaged the mob trying to form a ring to protect the building. It was too little too late. In the darkness and the frenzy, Keith and his four people had entered the main concourse and moved to the section on their left.

38

INHS Asvini – Breach

"What in god's name is happening down there? It's a war zone," said Tej looking down at the fire and smoke rising through the pouring rain. The quad was just coming in to land, and the scene below was frightening. The commander of the hospital security had finally ordered his men to fire at the crowd in front. He wasn't trained for crowd control, and shooting seemed to be the only option available. Smoke covered the front of the hospital, and multiple unidentifiable shadows seemed to be engaged in hand to hand fighting.

"Pilot, go towards the grounds at the back. Let us down there. Then go back and get the rest of the troops. Got it?" instructed ACP Shinde. "Check your guns and prepare to engage. Careful about civilians. My team and I will lead. Let the professionals handle this. The rest will stay back. Don't try to be heroes," he warned.

The copter swung over behind the buildings and landed softly on the grass. The six of them tumbled out and ran straight to the foyer, closely followed by the commandos from the second copter. A grisly sight of the two dead sailors greeted them.

There was a call from the shadows, and Keisham stepped out, his hands raised above his head. He had no wish to be shot down by the police in a case of mistaken identity.

"Major! It's me."

"What's happening here, Keisham?"

"There are two of them inside, sir. They're shooting up everything. I don't have a gun on me. I've been trying to help the wounded while trying to call you but couldn't get through."

"That means we're on track. They're here. Okay, we need to set up a perimeter to contain them inside. Then we'll wait for reinforcements."

"We don't have time for reinforcements, Shindeji. I know that is the standard operating procedure. But not in this situation. We need to tackle them now. God knows what they'll do once they realise they're cornered. We have the element of surprise and as Keisham says there are only two of the aliens."

Shinde made up his mind rapidly. "In that case - I want four teams. Two of you will go up front and cover the entrance. Keep away from the crowds. Get the aliens if they try to escape. Two more will remain here to cover the rear entrance. Shoot to kill. The rest will split up and follow us - one team left and the other to the right," Shinde instructed. The commandos split up into teams as directed. "You'd better come along with me, Major. Ma'am, you can lead the second team. Not my best choice but I agree, if we move fast, we may gain the upper hand. I'll get additional troops to you soon."

Rawat nodded and turned around. "You should stay here, Captain. I'll let you know when it's safe to enter."

"No way, Major. I'm going in with you. I'm responsible for getting Joe and Lucy into this situation and I can't step away now. End of discussion."

Tej rolled her eyes but said nothing as they raced into the building.

***

The screams from the wounded, and the dying hit their ears as soon as the double doors slid open. Many unmoving bodies lay on the floor, which was slick with blood. Intermittent gunfire rang out from their right, and the ACP, Ryan, and Rawat turned that way. The hospital facility had already been overwhelmed, and there was no one in sight to help the injured or engage the perpetrators. The sailors in the front were too busy managing the mob and were barely aware of the carnage inside.

Tej ran down the corridor to the left, followed by Abhiram, Anara, Keisham now armed, and one ATS commando. The sounds of the fighting outside grew muted as they went deeper into the building.

"Tej," said Anara, pulling at her sleeve. "If they're after Lucy and Joe, then we need to get to their room. They are helpless."

"Right, this floor looks empty. Let's go straight to the isolation room." Tej went to the bank of elevators, and one turned up as if on cue. They entered it and called out the sixth floor. It took mere seconds to make the trip. The doors of the elevator opened into another corridor. It was deathly quiet. Muted sounds of gunfire and quads flying outside could still be heard up here. This was interspersed with the soft sobbing of a woman.

The commando led from the front, followed by Keisham.

As they walked ahead cautiously, they found a nurse hiding behind a medical cart. Aisha looked unhurt and pointed towards the isolation room. *This is not what I wanted from the RE. So much death. What have I done?* They moved forward towards the isolation room just two doors further down the hallway.

The commando stopped beside the door with his back to the wall, gave a quick turn of his head and looked inside. The double pressure sealed doors did not allow him a good view. He motioned for them to stay behind, then rotated on his toes and kicked the first door open. As he fell inside, he found the emergency release and pushed it. The second door opened automatically, and he burst inside, catching a hail of bullets right on his chest. His body armour deflected a few but two found their mark, and he went down hard.

With a cry of rage Tej pulled out her gun, but Anara held it with her own hands. "No, don't! There are innocent people inside." Abhiram jumped across to the other side of the first door, his gun ready.

"Whoever you are inside. We don't want anyone else to get hurt. Put down your weapon and let's talk," Anara called out. Her heart was beating fast. She could never forgive herself if they had hurt Lucy.

"So…. it is you, Captain. I was hoping to see you again. Stay where you are. Otherwise, I will kill Lucy. You have done enough damage. This will end now."

Anara had heard that voice before. But where?

"You have the advantage over me then. I don't know who you are. Let me come inside, and I promise we'll talk."

"Have you already forgotten me, Captain Anara?" Biw mocked her. "Well, I haven't forgotten you. You destroyed my life, and for that, you will pay."

"I don't understand what you are saying. Look - just give me a chance, will you? We'll sort this out, and then you can return home."

"Ha! Do you really want me to believe you? You are a liar. I can never trust you. Not after what happened on HuZryss when you pulled that stunt, exploding the bombs and threatening everyone."

"Captain…" a frightened voice called out tremulously from inside the room.

"Lucy? Lucy! Are you all right?"

"Shut up!" Biw snarled. "One more word from you and your baby will die with you!"

"But she's your baby too, Jim!"

39

INHS Asvini - Standoff

Jur's headache was now threatening to overwhelm the senses. It had already lost count of the number of people it had killed. Still, the bloodlust was not satisfied. Killing nameless and faceless strangers was not enough anymore. Where were Lucy and Joe? It blundered around the corridor, took a turn and came to a stop. It was a dead end.

Shaking its head trying to get rid of the blinding pain, Jur turned around to find another way up. It turned back around the corner and stopped short once more. Five humans stood there blocking its path. Jur swung around the rifle and let loose another barrage in one smooth motion.

***

Have we taken a wrong turn somewhere? wondered Keith. *Did Aisha say turn right or turn left at the main doors? Where was she? Why was the ComNet not working? And all that shooting - God!* They'd better find the right room and get out of there before the police found them.

He and his team climbed up the stairs and walked down another corridor just like the ones on the floors below. They had nearly reached the end when they saw some movement around the corner. They hesitated for only one moment, but that was enough.

The last words in Keith's mind, before the bullets found their mark, were - *What in God's name is that creature?* All five of them crumpled to the floor. Keith's dreams of glory evaporated in one instance. Like that of many others that night, his death too was painful and pointless.

Jur looked down at the five dead men lying in front of it, mowed down by one burst of gunfire. Then it heard more shouting coming from the stairs, leading to the corridor. More people were coming up. *No problem. Tonight, was as good a time as any for the humans to die. I need to find my way back down and find Biw. Surely this is the wrong building.*

Jur kept his weapon pointed towards the stairs and shifted it into full auto laser mode. It would use more power, but it could only be the Earth military coming up now. *Who else would be foolish or brave enough to seek death?*

***

The ACP and others had been following the sound of the shooting. They had been avoiding the elevators and climbed up four flights of stairs. His instincts told him they were getting closer. A voice came through his earpiece; additional troops had landed, and the police had arrived as well. The situation in front was coming under control. The mob-frenzy had abated, and people were running away, leaving the injured and immobile behind on the ground, now strewn with dead bodies.

He saw a few civilians and doctors crouching behind an overturned trolley and called out, "Where are they?" There was no reply, and the people seemed to huddle closer. *Shell shock.*

He motioned to the team behind him to keep quiet and follow his lead and stepped cautiously up the last flight of stairs to take him to the next floor.

***

The ACP and Jur fired at each almost simultaneously, each missing the other by a whisker.

"Down! Get down! They're here!" Shinde shouted as he scrambled back to the relative safety of the staircase. The laser had just missed his helmet, and there was a deep hole with dark singed edges in the wall behind him.

"How many?" asked Rawat.

"I could see only one in the corridor - a bloody four-handed creature. The others may be hiding behind him. He's dressed in some sort of armour. Any of you carrying any tactical grenades?" He was cursing his haste in entering a combat situation with only hand weapons.

"I have one, sir," said the commando, removing one from his side belt and handing it over.

"Get your heads down," he warned as he chose the stun setting and threw the grenade.

***

Jur had already retreated behind the corner when the grenade flew towards it. The suit and helmet protected it completely. The optics went dark to protect it from the intense sound and flash from the grenade. It let loose a few more shots from the rifle when the heads-up display warned that weapon power was low. It was nearly out of bullets too. *Shouldn't have wasted it on all those stupid people!* Jur reached down and pulled out the trusted knife from its leg sheath. It would have to do. Jur peeped around the corner, just in time to see Shinde's head poke up from the stairs. Both ducked back quickly.

"Still only one and he's stopped firing? Why is that?"

"I'll go up, sir, and flush him out," said the commando.

"Easy now, soldier. Stay where you are. This is not the time for heroics. We have him cornered. Let him make the next move."

40

West Wing, INHS Asvini

It couldn't be! Not Jim! Why? The 'human' back on HuZryss. Joe and Lucy's friend. What is he doing here?

"Jim? Is that you? You are the mercenary?"

"Who's Jim? One of the humans from HuZryss?" asked Tej. "What's he doing here?"

"That's what I am trying to find out," Anara snapped.

"Yes, it is me, Captain. In the flesh, as you people like to say. I've come to pay you back. Don't try to enter - I have a device with me. If it explodes all of us will die together. I am not lying like you were, back on HuZryss. I have nothing to lose. Tell her, Doctor. Tell her what you see."

"He's serious, Captain. He has some kind of… of… bomb," the doctor called out.

"Okay. Okay. Keep calm, Doc. We'll get you out of there. Jim, please don't do anything rash, okay?"

She turned to see Tej calling for backup. Abhiram was still standing close to the door, his gun in hand and a determined expression on his face. Tej motioned him to wait for the backup to arrive. She prodded Anara. "Keep him talking," she mouthed the words.

"Jim, why are you doing this?"

"Funny you should ask that, Captain. What did you think would happen when you took my love and my child from me and left me behind in that godforsaken place? You took away from me the only family I have ever known!"

"Your love? Your child? But I thought Joe was the.... father?"

"Joe? The father?" he laughed. His voice was at a high pitch. "Joe was not the father. Lucy loves me!" His rage was at its peak now, blinding him to everything around him. All that mattered was revenge. Somebody had to pay for what had happened to him.

"No, Jim. I don't love you. Not anymore." Lucy's voice was suddenly stronger. "I loved you once. But then you changed, Jim. You changed and I could not be with you anymore. The TrueKifs saw you as weak, reached out and brainwashed you into their cause. The thought of unlimited power blinded you. You stopped thinking about all of us. I kept your secret, but once I knew I was pregnant, I could not bear the thought of my child growing up in your shadow. That's why I left HuZryss and start a new life."

"You didn't just leave me there, Lucy! You killed me on HuZryss. I have always loved you and this is how you repaid me? You took my child, Lucy!" He was screaming, and he no longer cared. "You took my respect. Without the Chairman I would not have had the courage to live. It gave me a chance to seek my revenge on the people of Earth." Jim spat on the ground. "I will take you back home with me. You will be mine and mine alone."

"Just look at yourself, Jim. I pity you. You have proven me

right. You cannot be a good father. You don't love me. You only love power. You desire what the chairman can offer you over me. I will never go back! Never!"

Jim's eyes glinted with a manic hatred. His hands shook with excitement and fury. He shook his head to clear the effect of the headache. "Then you will die here but my child will go with me. And no one… no one can stop me."

Tej saw an opportunity opening with Jim getting distracted. She moved aside to let Lieutenant Keisham come forward to the right of the door. Between the three of them, they should be able to overpower the bad guy.

They heard Jim move across the room and they distinctly heard a loud slap.

Several things happened at once. Both the doctor and Joe leaped forward at Jim, who staggered back under their combined weight. Abhiram and Keisham burst through the doors together, with Anara and Tej close behind.

Jim, Joe and the Doctor were struggling on the floor when a sharp whooshing sound was heard. Joe staggered back and fell against the bed, a singed hole in his chest. He was dead before his body hit the floor.

Jim threw the doctor off and fired more shots at those charging in from the door. Keisham held his fire for fear of hitting the wrong person. That was a mistake. One shot hit him in the neck and without the protection of body armour, he fell on his face. Tej moved instinctively to protect Anara, and a shot caught her in the shoulder spinning her around. She collapsed as well. Blood seeped on the floor and Lucy's screams filled the room.

Abhiram raised his gun but found that the doctor was in his way.

"Stop!" screamed Lucy from the bed - horrified at finding her friends getting hurt. "Please stop!"

Abhiram could react, Jim had jumped up, and he held his gun to the infant's head. "You move, she dies."

***

Jur was trapped. It removed the helmet and took a deep breath of the air on Earth. It put its head around the corner again. Just then Rawat peeked out from his hiding place. Their eyes met, and they recognized each other almost immediately. Jur exulted. *It's the military man from HuZryss. He was with Anara the whole time. Good. Revenge would be sweet.*

"Son of a…! It saw me. That's the leader of the TrueKif gang on HuZryss. It was a tough nut."

"You know him?" Rawat and Ryan nodded in affirmative. "What do we do about him?"

"Do about 'it'," Ryan reminded them. "They're hermaphrodites, remember? No gender differentiation. When are your troops coming in?"

"Any minute now. They have the location. We'll flush him out."

"Earthman? Major?" Jur's roar was a stark reminder of the menace facing them.

"Why is he… Why is it calling you?"

Rawat shrugged as the roar came again; this time bearing a challenge. "We have some unfinished business."

"Earthman! Why hide? Come fight."

Rawat closed his eyes. He should ignore it. He should wait for the troops. And yet-

He got up.

"Are you insane?" Shinde pulled him back down. "What the hell are you doing?"

"If I can end this now, we can avoid further bloodshed." Rawat had to keep his voice steady. To hide his fear but mainly to hide the rage, the rage that flared up with every memory of those three days, the rage that grew with every taunting cry from Jur.

The ACP, however, seemed at least partly aware of what was going on. He grabbed Rawat by the arms and looked directly into his eyes. "Listen to me," he said. "There is far more at stake here than your wounded pride."

"This isn't about pride anymore, sir. It's about revenge." Rawat pulled himself free of his grip and stood up, facing Jur fully.

There was a pounding in his ears matched only by that of his heart as he faced off with Jur. He forced himself to smile but found that it required little force. His anger saw to that.

"Well?" his voice was dangerously low. It sounded like it belonged to someone else.

Jur met Rawat's smile with its own. "Earthman. We meet again. You fight me."

"No weapons," Rawat said. "Hand to hand. Like men."

"Not men. Like KifrWyss." Jur dropped its weapon and without taking its eyes off Rawat, started pulling off its body armour, piece by piece, until it wore only blue pants, a knife sheathed at the waist. Somehow it seemed even more otherworldly and terrible like this; the skin was shining with sweat, the muscles bulging beneath scaled, dark green skin that barely contained them. It spread its four arms like a challenge, and as it did, it seemed to grow. Rawat felt his fists clench as the monster's smile turned into a snarl, a snarl that threatened to drag him back to those three days, a snarl that made him want to turn and run.

A snarl that made him that much more determined to win. Behind him, Ryan levelled Rawat's gun at Jur. Insurance, he supposed. He saw the rest of the troops do the same, yet no one was firing on the naked, vulnerable alien. The scene playing out had mesmerized them.

***

Rawat could feel time slowing around him, and as it did, he forced his breathing to be steady and his focus to sharpen. Fear, anger, revenge–there would be time for all of that later. At this moment these emotions were just obstacles he needed to overcome.

The moment is now.

With speed that belied its bulk, Jur lunged forward, barrelling towards Rawat with the speed and force of a freight train. Before the soldier could even get his arms up in a defensive position, two giant hands had closed around his throat. He tried to gasp but couldn't; the grip had cut off all air in seconds. His thoughts swam as Jur's snarl filled his vision and two spare hands grasped his before they could come to his defence.

His strength was failing, and he had to act fast. As the monster pulled him off the ground, he kicked as hard as he could, connecting with Jur's knee. It was no use. The creature didn't so much as flinch. And Rawat's vision was turning blurry.

Then, as Jur pulled Rawat closer, he slammed his head into the alien with all the force he had.

It hurt, but even in his ebbing focus, he could see the creature blink. That was all the encouragement he needed, and pain joined fear as he head-butted Jur again and again, until the alien yelped, and its grip loosened. Rawat took his chance, pulling his hands free, using them to push away from Jur as much as he could. He folded both his legs and kicked out hard. The grip on his neck vanished and, staggering, Rawat landed on his feet.

He backed away, trying to regain his focus, trying to catch his breath, but his enemy did not hesitate. Jur's foot was a blur at the bottom of his sight when Rawat felt his legs being knocked out from under him. He fell only to be caught by two enormous hands, hands that lifted him into the air and threw him as hard as he could against a nearby door.

Rawat was aware of the pain as the door gave way beneath the force of his flying body. He was aware of the impact as he hit the ground in what must have been a recovery room. He was acutely aware of the shape of Jur, towering over him and looking for the entire world like approaching death. But he was also aware of the firm voice in his head that told him he had to win this.

Rawat stood, only for the monster's foot to take him in the chest, sending him sprawling backward again.

This time he hit a wall but remaining upright was hardly an advantage as Jur was on him in seconds, raining down blow after blow. Rawat staggered, sagged and as Jur prepared to hit him again he brought his entire body upwards, letting the force carry his fist into the creature's chin and send it lurching backward, dazed.

It was all the advantage Rawat needed. He forgot reason or strategy or control as, with a strangled roar, he came at the monster, giving back as good as he got with blow after blow, relishing every hit he landed on Jur's face.

Shinde and Ryan had appeared in the door, but both paused at the sight. Ryan felt a vicious grin contort his face. *No insurance needed here.* Another strike and the creature fell back, landing hard on one of the hospital beds.

Behind Ryan and the ACP, the backup had arrived but none of them came any closer as, bloodied, beaten and breathing heavily, Rawat approached his feebly struggling enemy.

Then, faster than he could have anticipated, Jur pulled its knife from the sheath and swung it hard towards Rawat - catching him in the neck. As blood flowed freely from the wound, Rawat intercepted its wrist and twisted hard. Jur cried out, dropping the knife which Rawat caught in his spare hand. Memories flashed through his head. Memories of those three days, of all the shame he had suffered at the hands of these monsters. Held hostage; impotent.

No more.

Jur was staring up at him, eyes wide. It might have been fear. It might have been a final moment of respect for the human that had beaten it. Whatever it was, it didn't matter anymore. With his last remaining strength, Rawat brought the knife down, burying it to the hilt in the alien's chest.

It's over. Parakramo Vijayate.

Valour Triumphs.

41

East Wing, INHS Asvini

"Don't hurt her! Please don't hurt her!" screamed Lucy, as she tried getting up but the tubes inserted into her arms held her back. Jim threatened her to stay put while Anara looked upon all the people lying about hurt or dying. Her training took over as she analysed the tactical situation. With so many civilians in the room, the circumstances were probably not in favour of the good guys. She could see Abhiram keeping his weapon ready while texting instructions on his intercom. They needed to buy some time till the cavalry reached. She had to keep Jim talking and distracted.

"Don't do this Jim. She's your child!"

"Maybe it is time that I take what is rightfully mine, Captain Anara. I have consoled myself that this day will come when I will find my child. That is the only thought which has kept me sane. And now I am here and so are you. Stand back. You realise that I still have my device, don't you? You don't want to take any chances that would blow up this city and all of us."

Damn, damn, damn, thought Abhiram as he sent fresh instructions to his team.

"Look, Jim, I'm going to help these people who are hurt and then we're going to talk. Just put the gun down. You'll hurt someone."

"I want to hurt someone, Anara! I want to hurt all of you! Just like you hurt me and left me all alone!" Jim snapped. "Every single day since you left HuZryss, I have dreamed of the day when I would find you and take my revenge. No one is going to help anyone here. Let… them… die."

This isn't working; he's getting more volatile, thought Anara as she braced herself to end the confrontation. She didn't have a weapon, but Abhiram did, and he was unhurt.

"Don't think about it, Anara. The trigger is voice-activated. One word and BOOM," warned Jim. He had made up his mind. He knew how to hurt all these people. "I'm taking my daughter with me. We will return to HuZryss, and you will never find us again."

"No! No, you can't do that. You can't take my baby. Captain, please stop him!" implored Lucy as she struggled to get up again. The effort was too much, and she collapsed in a dead faint. Dr. Khan rushed to her ignoring the vicious look on Jim's face.

"Stand back from the door, Captain," said Jim as he put one hand under the child while keeping his eyes forward. Never having handled a child before, it was awkward for him, but he somehow got a decent grip. Baby Anara wailed loudly. Jim grew nervous, but this only made him more determined. *My daughter will come with me, and I will raise her in my image.* He kept his gun pointed at the child.

There was a commotion outside the door, and Abhiram

heaved a sigh of relief. The backup was here. He looked at Tej unconscious on the floor with blood seeping from the wound in her shoulder. He was ready to act, but the danger to the child and the threat of the device held him back. "Don't do anything rash. Wait for the opportunity," he called out to the team outside.

"You know you won't get out of this place, right? There are a hundred troops out there to stop you."

"Oh, they won't stop me. Not when I have the child in my hand and the bomb next to me."

"Oh, yeah? And how will you carry all of this on your own?"

Jim was caught for a moment before he realised what his best option would be. "I won't. The captain will carry it for me, won't you, Captain? Get up and take the child," he ordered.

Anara came forward and took the wailing baby in her arms. She rocked it a bit trying to soothe her but failed.

"Let's go now, Anara. Straight out the door. You go out first," Jim ordered Abhiram. "Clear the way and find us a mode of transport to get back to my ship. Remember, it will only take one word from me to blow the bomb."

There was no way out. They would play around for some more time and look for an opportunity. For now, they did as they were told. Abhiram exited first, keeping the double doors open. Anara went next, baby in her arms, Jim's gun on the baby's head and the device on Jim's back.

The soldiers in the corridor stepped back against the walls, clearing a small path for them to pass through. Their fingers were on their triggers, but the guns pointed down. The little procession walked out slowly, Jim continuously looking back and sideways - watchful of any threatening moves.

There was a clatter of steps, and new figures appeared in front. Ryan and the ACP had run all the way from the west wing leaving the local police behind to handle the dead alien. They halted, taking in the scene being played out in front of them. *Where's Rawat?* Anara wondered.

She caught Ryan's eyes, and he slowly shook his head, and Anara understood. Rawat was dead. She hoped he had died the way he'd lived - with courage and determination. But now was not the time to mourn him. She had an innocent life to protect. She hoped she would have Rawat's courage when her time came.

"Your partner is dead. You are alone now. Surrender while there is still time," called out the ACP.

"I hope it did not die without taking more humans with it. But as you can see, things are different here. Keep aside and don't come in my way. Go on, Anara," said Jim prodding her in the back with his gun.

Ryan saw the alertness in the Captain's eyes and was reassured that whatever her condition, she remained in control. She would find her way out of the predicament.

The group continued down the stairs and reached the main concourse. A scene of devastation greeted them. Medics, doctors, and EMRARs were on the scene helping those who were hurt. Collecting the dead bodies would come later. Everyone stopped working and looked up when the small group appeared at the head of the escalator.

Leaving the devastation behind, they went out the back exit which opened out to the lawn where two quadcopters were waiting. They entered the lead copter. Snipers on the roof and in other quadcopters flying above kept a close eye. They were looking for a chance to take a shot, but the three people were too close to each other. Even a slight error would have resulted in an innocent getting killed. The orders were explicit. Take no chances; wait for this to play out.

The group settled in, and Jim provided the coordinates to the pilot who took off and turned northwards. Jim sent a single coded message back to his ship asking them to be prepared.

42

The Return

"**S**witch off the virtual display and turn off auto-pilot. Just fly this thing manually," he ordered, pointing his gun at the pilot. "Tell them to clear the air of all aircraft. No one is to follow us. Understand?"

She did as commanded.

"This is Police 1-5-9 to Mumbai control," called out the pilot. "Be advised we are taking off now. We have two hostages on board. Request you to clear the airspace."

"Police 1-5-9–wilco. Please stand by."

The pilot increased power to the engines.

"Police 1-5-9–Mumbai control. On orders of the Commissioner of Police, I am ordering all other aircraft to stand down. You are clear."

"Roger, Mumbai Control," The pilot took off and deliberately flew slowly. Her instruments revealed clear airspace around their craft though there were multiple copters just at the edge of the range of her radar.

Jim looked through the windows at the ground below and saw thousands of people still lining the streets and some very large idols converging at the immersion points. Strangely, most other parts of the city were empty. The evacuation had been carried out successfully.

This will all end soon. I'll be a hero back home. I'm sure the Chairman will understand why I had to bring my baby back. If not, we will find some other place.

The baby had stopped wailing and now lapsed into sobs, still cradled in Anara's arms. She was angry at the pain the baby was undergoing and at her helplessness.

"You are hurting your baby, you know. Which father does that?"

"When she grows up, she'll understand this was for her own good." The baby's crying was getting on his nerves. "Can't you stop her crying? Silence her."

"You know nothing about babies, do you? I can't just ask her to shut up. She must be hungry, and she needs her mother," she stated firmly.

"Well, her mother is not here, so you'd better do your best." *Maybe this was not such a good idea after all. What do babies eat anyway? I've never even seen one before.*

Anara lapsed into silence trying to cradle the baby and keep her comfortable. She was also getting worried about the effect the atmosphere would have on the baby's frail body. *She should not have been taken out of the isolation chamber and yet here she was - flying off to God knows where at two thousand feet.* Anara looked out of the window to see the glass and steel skyscrapers rushing by. The air was clear of traffic. She turned when Jim coughed. His face was pale, and there were beads of sweat on his forehead. *What the hell now? Was he ill? I hope it's not contagious. Maybe the current situation required emotional action instead.*

"You don't look so well. What's wrong?"

"Nothing is wrong with me," he snapped then bent double as another racking cough hit him. However, his grip on the gun did not loosen. "Why can't you just keep quiet?"

"You need a doctor. You've not been using an isolation suit. Any of the bugs on Earth could have hurt you. Didn't you think of that?"

That's exactly what Jim was thinking. PiYena had assured them that the medications would take care of any eventuality. Well, it looked like this 'eventuality' was not covered. He was months away from KifrWyss and any doctors who could help him. No matter. He would survive.

"I guess you didn't, huh? Then I'm sure you did not think what would happen to your daughter in the open."

"What do you mean?" he asked, startled enough to forget his pain.

"Why do you think they kept her in the incubator, Jim? Why do you think Lucy was in isolation? Their bodies do not have immunity to Earth diseases. Just look at you now. What do you think will happen to your daughter in another few hours? Or even worse - what will happen to her when she is back on KifrWyss? Jim, as it is she's in a precarious position," Anara implored, using every ounce of persuasion she could muster. "I implore you. Don't make it worse for her. She cannot survive on Earth or on your planet without our help. Don't do this to her. She's your flesh and blood."

Was she right? I have seen what happened to Jur and me. Can the same thing happen to my daughter? She looks so weak - how was he going to take care of her on the spaceship? Jim hesitated, doubts clouded his mind, and his body betrayed him. He kept silent and did not reply.

"You've done enough damage to your home planet today Jim. So many people died. So many of them were wounded. It's time you stopped."

"This is not my home! Don't you understand that? It was never my home. You abandoned us - all of you. You left us to die in space!" He felt spent. The next word came out sullen rather than angry. "There is nothing for me here on Earth."

"You're wrong. You have Lucy, and you have your daughter. If you want, we can try to find your parents too."

Jim laughed but with bitterness. "Didn't you hear what Lucy said, Captain? She doesn't want me anymore, and if what you say is true, then my daughter may not have much time to live either. No, my time on Earth is over."

"We're in sight of the coordinates provided. What do you want me to do?" It was the pilot calling out from the controls.

Jim looked out but could not recognise the place - it was dark, and he'd never seen it from the air. His instrument, however, told him he had arrived.

"Land here," he instructed, and the pilot skilfully landed them next to the abandoned factory.

"Let's go, Captain. The ride is over." Jim opened the door and stepped out. Anara followed with the baby in her arms. Jim motioned the pilot also to get down and join them.

He pointed Anara forward, and they hastened forward to find the door and enter the dark structure.

"*Grakyss?*" a voice inquired from the darkness.

"*Pu rytss* Biw!" Jim answered, stating his identity. He pushed them forward as a light came on and they could see the TrueKif ship. It looked ready to go. Anara was looking for options to break free, but at the same time, she wanted to wait. She was getting the feeling that Jim was in two minds.

"Start the ship," Jim ordered.

"Where is Jur?"

"Jur gave up its life for the TrueKif. It is not coming back. And you'd better hurry if you don't want to spend your life in a human jail here on Earth."

That galvanized the pilot into action. It turned around rapidly and entered the ship.

"What's your final decision, Jim?" Anara braced herself for action and hoped her pilot would be ready to follow her lead. She was, however, still not sure how to protect the baby. "I'll give you a choice. Take me with you. I'll be your hostage. Leave your daughter here where she will be safe."

Jim stood still for such a long time that she wondered if he'd even heard her. Then he turned around slowly, and she was shocked to see tears in his eyes. The human in him had won.

"Maybe you are right, Captain Anara. Maybe I am not ready to be a father. I will never forgive Lucy or you for what you have done, but I cannot allow my daughter to be hurt. Keep her with you, Anara and keep her safe. Tell her that her father tried to be good, but he failed." He touched the baby's cheeks gently gazing at the face wet with tears. Then he turned around and walked into the ship, closing the door firmly behind him.

The engines came to life with a roar. Anara and the pilot ran to find shelter. As they cowered behind a large pillar, the ship took off, drowning them in noise and dust.

They rushed out of the building and stood to watch as the ship gained speed rapidly and almost immediately vanished from view among the clouds, the roar of other crafts assailed their ears, as several other aircrafts screamed overhead, in hot pursuit.

Disturbed by all the noise, baby Anara woke up and started crying again. Anara saw her face and the tiny clenched fist and then looked up to the sky - *Goodbye, Jim. I hope you can find some peace.*

EPILOGUE

Time passed in a blur. He did not even realise that a few weeks had already gone by. The ship's flight at the speed of light had enabled them to evade the hyper-ships, which had tried to intercept them. They had escaped from Earth. But Jim was sure *Antariksh* and Anara would pursue him.

He had not spoken to anyone on board since the day they had left Earth. He stayed in his room, weakened by whatever bacteria or virus that had invaded his body. His medication had controlled the fever but there was no cure. His body was racked with pain, and now he could taste blood in his mouth.

The sense of failure overwhelmed him but coming to terms with the loss of his daughter preyed on his mind. He could not bear it anymore. This had to end now. There was only one way.

He got up slowly from his bed and walked to the device hoping it was still working. He caressed it like it was his only friend. Then uttered a single word - *Brikshuv!* The weapon became energised, and a control panel appeared. There was only one button. He caressed the button gently, lovingly reliving the face of his daughter and without hesitating further, pressed it.

It is done. Goodbye Lucy! Goodbye, my baby!

He didn't even hear the weapon exploding. He evaporated in an instant - along with the TrueKif ship which was travelling at the speed of light. The fusion reactors on the ship also exploded simultaneously in sympathetic detonation and a huge fireball formed.

But this was nothing compared to the explosion as the matter-antimatter tanks buckled. The colossal detonation at light speed was enough to tear a hole in the very fabric of space-time. A rupture - a naked singularity - a black hole - formed in space with the power to devour everything it encountered.

Nothing would escape its gravitational pull. Not planets. Not suns. Not even light.

DEAR READER,

If you enjoyed this book, please take a few moments to write a review on Amazon and Goodreads. Thank you!
You can sign up for my mailing list for exclusive content and new releases at www.kumarlauthor.com.